COMPANY / ILL SEEN ILL SAID /
WORSTWARD HO / STIRRINGS STILL

Dirk Van Hulle (Centre for Manuscript Genetics, University of Antwerp) is co-director of the Beckett Digital Manuscript Project and the author of *Manuscript Genetics: Joyce's Know-How, Beckett's Nohow*. He is currently preparing an electronic genetic edition of *Stirrings Still/Soubresauts*.

Titles in the Samuel Beckett series

ENDGAME
Preface by Rónán McDonald
COMPANY/ILL SEEN ILL SAID/WORSTWARD HO/STIRRINGS STILL
Edited by Dirk Van Hulle
KRAPP'S LAST TAPE AND OTHER SHORTER PLAYS
Preface by S. E. Gontarski
MURPHY
Edited by J. C. C. Mays
WATT
Edited by C. J. Ackerley

Forthcoming titles

MORE PRICKS THAN KICKS
Edited by Cassandra Nelson
ALL THAT FALL AND OTHER PLAYS FOR RADIO AND SCREEN
Preface by Everett Frost
MOLLOY
Edited by Shane Weller
MALONE DIES
Edited by Peter Boxall
THE UNNAMABLE
Edited by Steven Connor
HOW IT IS
Edited by Magessa O'Reilly
HAPPY DAYS
Preface by James Knowlson
THE EXPELLED/THE CALMATIVE/THE END/FIRST LOVE
Edited by Christopher Ricks
WAITING FOR GODOT
Preface by Mary Bryden
TEXTS FOR NOTHING/RESIDUA/FIZZLES: SHORTER FICTION 1950–1981
Edited by Mark Nixon
MERCIER AND CAMIER
Edited by Sean Kennedy
SELECTED POEMS 1930–1988
Edited by David Wheatley

SAMUEL BECKETT

Company
Ill Seen Ill Said
Worstward Ho
Stirrings Still

Edited by Dirk Van Hulle

faber and faber

This edition first published in 2009
by Faber and Faber Ltd
Bloomsbury House
74–77 Great Russell Street
London WC1B 3DA

Company originally published as *Compagnie*, Les Éditions de Minuit 1980; first
published in Great Britain by John Calder Publishers 1980.
Ill Seen Ill Said originally published as *Mal vu mal dit*, Les Éditions de Minuit 1981;
first published in Great Britain by John Calder Publishers 1982.
Worstward Ho first published in Great Britain by John Calder Publishers 1983.
Stirrings Still first published in Great Britain by John Calder Publishers 1988;
reprinted in *As the Story Was Told*, John Calder Publishers 1990.
One Evening originally published as *Un Soir*, Les Éditions de Minuit 1980;
first published in Great Britain in *JOBS* 6, 1980; reprinted in *As the Story was Told*,
John Calder Publishers 1990.
The Way first published in Great Britain by Faber & Faber 2009.
Ceiling first published in Great Britain by Thames & Hudson in *Arikha*
(Richard Channin and others) 1985.
What is the Word (a translation of *Comment dire*) first published in Great Britain
by the *Sunday Correspondent* 1989; reprinted in *As The Story was Told*,
John Calder Publishers 1990.
Heard in the Dark 1 first published in Great Britain by John Calder Publishers
in *New Writing and Writers 17*, 1980; reprinted in *As the Story was Told*,
John Calder Publishers 1990.
Heard in the Dark 2 first published in Great Britain by John Calder Publishers
in *JOBS* 5, 1979; reprinted in *As the Story was Told*, John Calder Publishers 1990.

Typeset byRefineCatch Limited, Bungay, Suffolk
Printed and bound by CPI Group (UK) Ltd, Croydon, CR0 4YY

A CIP record for this book
is available from the British Library

ISBN 978-0-571-24473-7

2 4 6 8 10 9 7 5 3

Contents

Preface

On the back of one of his manuscripts, Samuel Beckett calcu-
lated in 1977 how long he had been dying: approximately
600,000 hours since his birth on Good Friday 1906. There
were, as it happened, approximately 100,000 hours to go.
During this last decade, from *Company* in 1980 to *Stirrings Still*
in 1989, Beckett wrote four of the most moving and unsettling
prose works of the twentieth century, which form the core of the
present edition. *Company*, *Ill Seen Ill Said* and *Worstward Ho*
appeared independently, and were subsequently brought
together by his publisher John Calder under the collective title
Nohow On (June 1989); *Stirrings Still* appeared separately in
April 1989.[1] During this last decade Beckett also wrote a
number of shorter prose texts, all of which are variously related
to the four major works. These are also included in the present
edition; the preface summarizes their different textual situa-
tions, following the order of composition, and pays attention to
the process of composition.

Company

In January 1977, Beckett started writing an unpublished prose
text known as 'The Voice' or 'Verbatim'.[2] Both titles appear on
the manuscript of *Company*, preserved at the University of
Reading.[3] The Voice, 'speaking of itself in the third person
singular', begins by saying that it will not cease 'till hearing
cease'. A close relationship between speaker and listener is inti-
mated. When a character does appear, it is a 'wayfarer' who has
been 'out since dawn plodding forward through the gloaming'.
There are other affinities with what was to become *Company*,
notably the references – 'for verisimilitude' – to Ballyogan Road

and Croker's Acres (close to Leopardstown racecourse and Foxrock, the suburb of Dublin where Beckett grew up), and the reference to a father's shade.

Beckett abandoned 'Verbatim' in May 1977, but salvaged a few snippets when he integrated this fragment of prose into the characteristic structure of *Company*, which consists of fifty-nine discrete paragraphs. A number of these are presented as reminiscences in the second person singular (as in the one-act play, *That Time,* written slightly earlier): 'Use of the second person marks the voice. That of the third that cankerous other' (para. 3). This 'other' is described elsewhere as 'Deviser of the voice and of its hearer and of himself. Deviser of himself for company', like the solitary child who turns himself into children, mentioned in *Endgame.* The narrator calls his 'hearer' M. Formerly, the thirteenth letter of the alphabet served as the first initial of Beckett's main characters, as in *Murphy, Mercier, Molloy, Malone,* devised for company. But as the last word of *Company* suggests the solitary man who turns himself into men is not Malone, rather 'Alone'.

According to John Calder, on its first appearance *Company* 'received more attention than any of Beckett's prose works since *Imagination Dead Imagine*' (fifteen years earlier), being read by Patrick Magee on BBC radio and performed in a dramatized version at the National Theatre. It has been suggested by John Banville that the relative popularity of *Company* 'can at least in part be explained by the air of nostalgia that pervades it.'[4] Aside from its many charged references to Beckett's early life, *Company* is also a palimpsest of allusions to and echoes of his earlier work, as well as to the work of others, all of which form part of the text's company.

Writing the final pages seems to have proved unusually difficult, and included an abortive attempt to graft a passage from *A Piece of Monologue* (itself in mid-composition), but by the end of July 1979 *Company* was finished. It was Beckett's first major prose text in English since *From an Abandoned Work* (1956), and he started translating it into French on 3 August. After two years of composition, the translation as such took only twenty-four days. The French text was the first to be published (7 January 1980), and by the time the English version came out later in the same year, it had been revised in the light of *Compagnie* (published by Editions de Minuit).[5] Although Beckett generally proof-read his late texts carefully, he did mention afterwards in a letter to Martha Fehsenfeld (18 November 1980) that 'philogenitiveness' in para. 51 should read 'philoprogenitiveness', which is how it appears in the present edition.

Two of the longest paragraphs of *Company* had been published independently: para. 39 as 'Heard in the Dark 1' in *New Writing and Writers* 17 (Calder, 1980) and para. 40 as 'Heard in the Dark 2' in *Journal of Beckett Studies* 5 (Autumn 1979). They contain minor variants. For instance in 'Heard in the Dark 2', when the boy tries to imitate his father's chuckle the father is 'amused', whereas in *Company* he is 'tickled'. Paras. 39 and 40 take their place in the structure of *Company*, but also have a separate self-contained existence, and an independent publication history; they are included here as an appendix.

One Evening

On 3 October 1979 Beckett's friend Con Leventhal died. He had replaced Beckett as an instructor at Trinity College in Dublin half a century earlier, and married Beckett's muse Ethna MacCarthy (the 'Alba' of *Dream of Fair to Middling Women*), and his death may have played a role in the genesis of *Un Soir*. The starting point of the French text, written on 24 October, is of a man lying on the ground, stumbled upon by an old woman in search of wild yellow flowers to decorate the grave of her dead husband. Not unlike Hamm's chronicle in *Endgame*, the narrative is repeatedly interrupted by the narrator's notes to himself. 'All that seems to hang together,' he concludes: 'But no more about it.'

Beckett translated the text into English in the first week of November 1979, and *One Evening* was published in the *Journal of*

Beckett Studies 6 (Autumn 1980). It has been read as an early version of the opening of *Ill Seen Ill Said*, notably in the shared use of prompts, or phrases spoken as if to camera. In this sense it is comparable to 'Heard in the Dark 2', but whereas the latter is an extract from work in progress on *Company*, *One Evening* stands in a far more independent relation to *Ill Seen Ill Said*. After its first publication it appeared subsequently in *art press* 51 (September 1981) and in *New Writers and Writing* 20 (Calder, 1983).

Ill Seen Ill Said

If *Company* may be described as partly autobiographical, *Ill Seen Ill Said* has as its main character an old woman. Narrated in the third person, its sixty-one unnumbered paragraphs in French can be seen as a counterpart to *Company* with its not-quite sixty paragraphs written in English. The original French manuscript, however, consisted of sixty-four numbered fragments, suggesting a chessboard structure. In an exercise notebook Beckett drew up an outline which succinctly labels the contents of each paragraph. He began translating *Mal vu mal dit* on 10 December 1980, even as the French original was still being written and revised (between October 1979 and January 1981). On the first page of the English manuscript, the text was provisionally titled 'The Evening or the Night'. The translation was completed in one month and on the last page Beckett inscribed the definitive title 'Ill Seen Ill Said'. It was first published complete in the *New Yorker* (5 October 1981), and subsequently in volume-form by Grove Press (1981).[6] The first English trade edition appeared from Calder in 1982, and the text was performed on BBC Radio 3 by Patrick Magee in September 1982.[7]

As in all of these late works, Shakespeare is never far away. The French 'oeil las' (para. 51) was originally translated as 'weary eye' but in the second typescript Beckett replaced it by 'vile jelly', referring to the moment in *King Lear* when Gloucester is blinded. The revision coincided with Beckett's copying a few lines from *King Lear* into the so-called 'Sottisier' notebook – lines spoken by Gloucester's son and relating to his blind father's lament: 'I have no way.' This 'no way' is the background against which Beckett's next text took shape.

The Way

This short prose text was written in mid-May 1981, between two trips to Stuttgart, where Beckett was helping the Süddeutsche Rundfunk production of *Quad*, his wordless 'ballet' for television (whose geometrical quincunx can be seen as combining the two signs which announce respectively the two paragraphs of *The Way*: 8 and ∞). As Beckett indicated on the manuscript, *The Way* was a provisional title. Nonetheless it is generally preferred to 'Criscross to Infinity', the title 'foisted on Beckett'[8] for the work's publication in *College Literature* 8, no. 3 (1981).

The route describes the shape of an infinity symbol, from foot to crown and back. An addition to the first manuscript version specifies: 'The two ways were one way', in reference to Beckett's old philosophical notes on the Presocratics, notably a fragment of Heraclitus quoted in John Burnet's *Greek Philosophy* (1914): 'The way up and the way down [are] one and the same [. . .] Fire, water, earth is the way down, and earth, water, fire is the way up. And these two ways are forever being traversed in opposite directions at once.' Beckett had already made irreverent use of this philosophical trope fifty years earlier in *Dream of Fair to Middling Women*, where Belacqua discovers the line of the 'drink graph' looping back on itself like an eight: 'if you had got what you were looking for on the way up you got it again on the way down. The bumless eight of the drink figure. You did not end up where you started, but coming down you met yourself going up.'[9]

So, while *The Way* can be read as a realistic description of a 'wayfarer' in a familiar Beckettian landscape, or calvary, it is also the brief translation of a philosophical metaphor and a way of thought: 'Well on the way to inexistence,' in the words of *Ill Seen Ill Said*: 'as to zero the infinite.'

Ceiling

The way was paved for this brief text by Beckett's
shortest poem, written on 9 April 1981 in the 'Sottisier'
notebook:

Ceiling

lid eye bid
byebye

No sooner have the eyes opened than the business of dying
sets in. In July 1981, Beckett wrote a prose *Ceiling*, provisionally titled 'On Coming to' in the manuscript. The point
of departure for *Ceiling* had been reached as early as *Murphy*
in the 1930s: 'When he came to, or rather from, how he
had no idea, the first thing he saw was the fug.'[10] In *Ceiling* this
premise becomes a study of consciousness as a return to
consciousness, as consciousness regained. Intended as a contri-
bution to a monograph devoted to the painter, Avigdor Arikha,
Beckett completed a first version in Courmayeur on 10 July
1981, and a second version in Paris dated 26 July 1981.
On 7 September he gave the typescript to the painter's
wife Anne Atik (who reproduces it in her memoir *How it
Was*, 2001), with the superscription "for Avigdor/September
1981"; the original title was crossed out, with *Somehow again*
substituted by pen. Eventually the title reverted to *Ceiling*. Anne
Atik notes that Beckett 'had planned to write about A.'s work
for him, but decided to write a text about seeing, instead, which
became *Ceiling*, as having much more to do with A.'s
approach'.[11] No French version was undertaken by Beckett.
Ceiling was first published in *Arikha* (Richard Channin and
others; Hermann, Paris, and Thames & Hudson, London,
1985), thereafter in the book-catalogue *Avigdor Arikha: From
Life: Drawings and Prints 1965–2005*, edited by Duncan Thomson
and Stephen Coppel (the British Museum Press, 2006), and
latterly in *Fulcrum* 6 (Boston, 2008) with a note by Christopher
Ricks.

Worstward Ho

Two weeks after finishing *Ceiling* Beckett began the first draft
of *Worstward Ho*, on 9 August 1981. As the provisional title
Better Worse indicates, this work can be read as a set of
staccato variations on the Shakespearian theme that 'The
worst is not / So long as one can say, This is the worst.' (as
copied out in the 'Sottisier' notebook). The idea of being 'Well
on the way to inexistence' is further elaborated in the so-called
'Worstward Poems' at the back of the first manuscript of
Worstward Ho, which precede two schematic drawings of
the scenic movements in *Quad*. Two of these 'Worstward
Poems' are variations on the theme 'on whence / no sense / but
on / to whence / no sense'. These are followed by a so-called
'Poetic miscalculation':

> from y to z
> 95.1 %
> to the dearest decimal dead
> incalescent

The notion of getting hotter – incalescent – or of being close to
the 'worst' but not quite there yet, characterizes Beckett's late
texts, but in *Worstward Ho* it is explicitly acted out in language.
As the line from *King Lear* indicates, the word 'worst' is inade-
quate, for as long as it can be uttered, the situation can worsen.
This challenge is the greatest paradox for the writer.

Since a spoken or written 'worst' cannot be the absolute
worst, some aspects of the transmission of this text also touch
on its thematic core, not least the variants between 'worse' (final
typescript) and 'worst' (Calder) in para. 61. The American
Grove (1983) and Calder text (1983) differ in six instances,
analysed by Ruud Hisgen and Adriaan van der Weel.[12]
According to John Calder, discrepancies between the final
typescript and the Calder edition are probably the result of revi-
sions made by Beckett in proof, but unfortunately the proofs are
lost. The author's final typescript (preserved at the Fonds John

Calder, IMEC, Normandy) has been followed as the base text for the present edition.

Stirrings Still

Beckett's last independent prose work was written in English and French between 1983 and 1987. The text of the limited edition of *Stirrings Still* contains one error ('withersoever' instead of 'whithersoever'), pointed out to Beckett by the actor Barry McGovern, and immediately corrected by the author in McGovern's copy, which may therefore serve as a base text, rather than the initial newspaper publication in the *Guardian* and *Irish Independent* (3 March 1989), or in the *Manchester Guardian* (19 March 1989). Apart from a few textual errors, the text in the *Guardian* is subdivided into four instead of three sections. The version in the *Irish Independent* is punctuated by cartoons, as in the case of the publication of *Ill Seen Ill Said* in the *New Yorker*, whereas the limited edition is illustrated with lithographs by Louis le Brocquy. *Stirrings Still* was thereafter collected with other uncollected late texts in *As the Story Was Told* (Calder 1990). It was dedicated to Barney Rosset, who had been dismissed as chief editor at Grove Press in April 1986.[13] By way of helping him, Beckett was stimulated to revise two previously written fragments of prose and eventually to add a third, to produce the work that became *Stirrings Still*.

The title draws on para. 26 of *Company*: 'Pangs of faint light and stirrings still. Unformulable gropings of the mind. Unstillable.' The genesis of *Stirrings Still* – with its reiterated Beckettian theme of a man seeing himself rise and disappear – was long and complex, including uncertainty as to which language to use. On the first manuscript page (dated 27 June 1983), Beckett began with a 'fragment' in French, which he then reworked in English. Whereas the second page opens with an English paragraph, followed by a new attempt in French. Eventually Beckett opted for English. The exercise book containing early drafts of *Stirrings Still* also features two abandoned dramatic fragments referring to Shakespeare's sonnets. There are spectral references to Beckett's life, for example in the allusion to Arthur Darley ('Darly'), his doctor-friend from his days with the Irish Red Cross in Normandy in 1945, who was to die of tuberculosis a few years later. Among the more explicit references in the text is an allusion to Beckett's favourite poem by the medieval German poet Walther von der Vogelweide, which describes the poet sitting on a stone and considering how one should live on this earth. But the most remarkable reference is a concealed allusion to Beckett's life-long master, Dante.

In the last of the text's three numbered sections, the protago-nist hears something 'from deep within', a sentence containing one word he cannot distinguish: 'oh how *and here a word he could not catch* it were to end where never till then'. He cannot catch the word because it is too 'faint'. When Beckett had written 'faint' in his manuscript on the right-hand side of his notebook, this apparently reminded him of an Italian phrase, which he wrote down on the left-hand page: 'per lungo silenzio fioco' – immediately followed by a translation, hesitating between 'faint' or 'hoarse from long silence'. This passage, from the opening canto of the *Divina Commedia*, describes how the guide Virgil appears to Dante, just before the poet calls him 'maestro'. Beckett subsequently considered replacing the word 'faint' in the draft by 'hoarse from long silence' but decided against it, and stuck to 'faint'. So at the surface level eventually nothing changes and in the published version there is no direct indica-tion of a link with Dante. Nonetheless, its presence in the manuscripts indicates a Dantean dimension that may be relevant in the search for 'that missing word'.

what is the word

what is the word is Beckett's translation of *Comment dire*, a fifty-three-line poem which constitutes his last published writing. 'Quel est le mot?' was still the pressing question when he was in the Hôpital Pasteur, and then in the nursing home *Le Tiers Temps*, in July 1988. On the first manuscript page he changed the key line from 'quel est le mot—' to 'comment dire—' followed by hyphens, or what he called 'traits de désunion'. On 29 October he wrote out a fair copy, a facsimile edition of which was produced for the *librairie Compagnie* in May 1989. The French text appeared in the literature section of the newspaper *Libération* on 1 June 1989 under the heading 'Un poème inédit'.

Beckett's English translation was published posthumously in the *Irish Times* (25–27 December 1989) and a few days later in the *Sunday Correspondent* (31 December). A version with the dedication 'for Joe Chaikin' was published in *Grand Street* vol. 9, no. 2 (Winter 1990). The text reproduced here is the final, word-processed version, a photocopy of which is preserved at the University of Reading (UoR MS 3506).

The English version was included both in *As the Story Was Told: Late and Uncollected Prose* (Calder, and Riverrun Press, 1990) and in *Poems 1930–1989* (Calder, 2002).[14] Within the present Faber readers' edition, *what is the word* will be published in the volume dedicated to Beckett's poetry. It also finds its place in the present volume, because Beckett's late texts defy traditional generic labelling, and because this last text was consciously written as an end-piece. With its subtle allusion to the last line of the final work by his mentor James Joyce ('afaint afar away'), and its failure to find the word for what is 'over there', Beckett concluded his whole oeuvre in mid-sentence, as an unfinished work in progress. On the first page of the manuscript of *what is the word*, he added in the top margin 'Keep ! for end', indicating that, no matter how much longer he might live and whatever he might still write, the final word had to be this acknowledgement that he could not find the word.

PREFACE

Notes

1 For an account of the origins of *Nohow On*, and a critique of its rationale as a collection or 'trilogy', see John Banville, 'The Last Word', *New York Review of Books*, 39:14, 13 August 1992. According to Calder, Beckett suggested adding *Stirrings Still*, as a fourth text, but *Nohow On* was already in press.

2 For the dating of crucial moments in the composition of Beckett's late texts, I owe a debt of gratitude to the following: John Pilling, *A Samuel Beckett Chronology* (New York: Palgrave MacMillan, 2006), Ruby Cohn, *A Beckett Canon* (Ann Arbor: University of Michigan Press, 2001) and *The Faber Companion to Samuel Beckett* (London: Faber and Faber, 2006) by C. J. Ackerley and S. E. Gontarski.

3 A transcription appears in Charles Krance's bilingual variorum edition of *Company/Compagnie* and *A Piece of Monologue/Solo* (New York: Garland, 1993).

4 John Banville, 'The Last Word', op. cit.

5 In a letter to Ruby Cohn, Beckett mentioned on 10 April 1980 that he had corrected the proofs for the UK (Calder) edition of *Company*. The Calder text differs slightly from the American (Grove) edition, as follows: 'complement' (Calder) instead of 'adjunct' (Grove) in para. 6; 'how far more likely' (Calder) instead of 'how more likely' (Grove) in para. 38; 'adjunction' (Calder) instead of 'addition' (Grove) in para. 54; 'rise again' (Calder) instead of 'rise to your arse again' (Grove) in the penultimate paragraph – 'to your arse' deleted on the Calder proofs). The present edition follows the Calder proofs, corrected by Beckett in March–April 1980.

6 The corrected typescript (version 'e' in Charles Krance's variorum edition) differs from the first publication in the *New Yorker* in a few instances, such as 'Rid of' [typescript]/'Shut of' [*New Yorker*] in para. 3; 'no less solitude' [typescript]/'no lesser solitude' [*New Yorker*] in para. 31; 'two black blanks' [typescript]/'too black blanks' [*New Yorker*] in para. 59 ('two' is an autograph correction on the typescript). The text of the *New Yorker* differs in places from the first edition in book form (Grove): the variant 'from down on her knees' [*New Yorker*]/ 'from off her knees' [Grove] in para. 8 is one of the few instances where the text of the *New Yorker* deviates from the base text of the present edition. For the consultation of the corrected typescript I owe a debt of gratitude to James Knowlson.

7 Charles Krance's bilingual edition of *Ill Seen Ill Said* (Garland, 1996) contains a synoptic account of its textual genesis.

8 Ruby Cohn, *A Beckett Canon* (Ann Arbor: University of Michigan Press, 2001), 369.

9 Samuel Beckett, *Dream of Fair to Middling Women* (Dublin: The Black Cat Press, 1992), 226.

10 Samuel Beckett, *Murphy* (New York: Grove Press, 1957), 191.

11 Anne Atik, *How it Was: A Memoir of Samuel Beckett* (London: Faber and Faber, 2001), 108.

12 Ruud Hisgen and Adriaan van de Weel, *The Silencing of the Sphinx* (Leiden: privately printed, 1998), 66–7.

13 James Knowlson, *Damned to Fame: The Life of Samuel Beckett* (London: Bloomsbury, 1996), 699.

14 Shane Weller has argued against treating the text as a piece of prose: 'The Word Folly: Samuel Beckett's *Comment dire (what is the word)*', Angelaki 5:1 (April 2000), 165–80; 175 note 2.

Table of Dates

[Note: where unspecified, translations from French to English or vice versa are by Beckett]

1906

13 April   Samuel Beckett [Samuel Barclay Beckett] born at 'Cooldrinagh', a house in Foxrock, a village south of Dublin, on Good Friday, the second child of William Beckett and May Beckett, née Roe; he is preceded by a brother, Frank Edward, born 26 July 1902.

1911

Enters kindergarten at Ida and Pauline Elsner's private academy in Leopardstown.

1915

Attends larger Earlsfort House School in Dublin.

1920

Follows Frank to Portora Royal, a distinguished Protestant boarding school in Enniskillen, County Fermanagh (soon to become part of Northern Ireland).

1923

October   Enrolls at Trinity College, Dublin (TCD) to study for an Arts degree.

1926

August   First visit to France, a month-long cycling tour of the Loire Valley.

1927

April–August   Travels through Florence and Venice, visiting museums, galleries, and churches.

December   Receives B.A. in Modern Languages (French and Italian) and graduates first in the First Class.

1928

Jan.–June	Teaches French and English at Campbell College, Belfast.
September	First trip to Germany to visit seventeen-year-old Peggy Sinclair, a cousin on his father's side, and her family in Kassel.
1 November	Arrives in Paris as an exchange *lecteur* at the École Normale Supérieure. Quickly becomes friends with his predecessor, Thomas MacGreevy, who introduces Beckett to James Joyce and other influential Anglophone writers and publishers.
December	Spends Christmas in Kassel (as also in 1929, 1930, and 1931).

1929

June	Publishes first critical essay ('Dante . . . Bruno. Vico . . Joyce') and first story ('Assumption') in *transition* magazine.

1930

July	*Whoroscope* (Paris: Hours Press).
October	Returns to TCD to begin a two-year appointment as lecturer in French.
November	Introduced by MacGreevy to the painter and writer Jack B. Yeats in Dublin.

1931

March	*Proust* (London: Chatto and Windus).
September	First Irish publication, the poem 'Alba' in *Dublin Magazine*.

1932

January	Resigns his lectureship via telegram from Kassel and moves to Paris.
Feb.–June	First serious attempt at a novel, the posthumously published *Dream of Fair to Middling Women*.
December	Story 'Dante and the Lobster' appears in *This Quarter* (Paris).

TABLE OF DATES

1933

3 May
Death of Peggy Sinclair from tuberculosis.

26 June
Death of William Beckett from a heart attack.

1934

January
Moves to London and begins psychoanalysis with Wilfred Bion at the Tavistock Clinic.

February
Negro Anthology, edited by Nancy Cunard and with numerous translations by Beckett (London: Wishart and Company).

May
More Pricks Than Kicks (London: Chatto and Windus).

Aug.–Sept.
Contributes several stories and reviews to literary magazines in London and Dublin.

1935

November
Echo's Bones and Other Precipitates, a cycle of thirteen poems (Paris: Europa Press).

1936

Returns to Dublin.

29 September
Leaves Ireland for a seven-month stay in Germany.

1937

Apr.–Aug.
First serious attempt at a play, *Human Wishes*, about Samuel Johnson and his circle.

October
Settles in Paris.

1938

6/7 January
Stabbed by a street pimp in Montparnasse. Among his visitors at L'Hôpital Broussais is Suzanne Deschevaux-Dumesnil, an acquaintance who is to become Beckett's companion for life.

March
Murphy (London: Routledge).

April
Begins writing poetry directly in French.

1939

3 September
Great Britain and France declare war on Germany. Beckett abruptly ends a visit to Ireland and returns to Paris the next day.

1950

25 August   Death of May Beckett.

1951

March   *Molloy*, in French (Paris: Les Éditions de Minuit).

November   *Malone meurt* (Paris: Minuit).

1952

               Purchases land at Ussy-sur-Marne, subsequently Beckett's preferred location for writing.

September   *En attendant Godot* (Paris: Minuit).

1953

5 January   Premiere of *Godot* at the Théâtre de Babylone in Montparnasse, directed by Roger Blin.

May   *L'Innommable* (Paris: Minuit).

August   *Watt*, in English (Paris: Olympia Press).

1954

8 September   *Waiting for Godot* (New York: Grove Press).

13 September   Death of Frank Beckett from lung cancer.

1955

March   *Molloy*, translated into English with Patrick Bowles (New York: Grove; Paris: Olympia).

3 August   First English production of *Godot* opens in London at the Arts Theatre.

November   *Nouvelles et Textes pour rien* (Paris: Minuit).

1956

3 January   American *Godot* premiere in Miami.

February   First British publication of *Waiting for Godot* (London: Faber).

October   *Malone Dies* (New York: Grove).

1957

January   First radio broadcast, *All That Fall* on the BBC Third Programme.

               Fin de partie, suivi de Acte sans paroles (Paris: Minuit).

28 March   Death of Jack B. Yeats.

May	Assists with the German production of *Play* (*Spiel*, translated by Elmar and Erika Tophoven) in Ulm.
22 May	Outline of *Film* sent to Grove Press. *Film* would be produced in 1964, starring Buster Keaton, and released at the Venice Film Festival the following year.

1964

March	*Play and Two Short Pieces for Radio* (London: Faber).
April	*How It Is*, translation of *Comment c'est* (London: Calder; New York: Grove).
June	*Comédie*, translation of *Play*, in *Les Lettres nouvelles*.
July–Aug.	First and only trip to the United States, to assist with the production of *Film* in New York.

1965

October	*Imagination morte imaginez* (Paris: Minuit).
November	*Imagination Dead Imagine* (London: *The Sunday Times*, Calder).

1966

January	*Comédie et Actes divers*, including *Dis Joe* and *Va et vient* (Paris: Minuit).
February	*Assez* (Paris: Minuit).
October	*Bing* (Paris: Minuit).

1967

February	*D'un ouvrage abandonné* (Paris: Minuit). *Têtes-mortes* (Paris: Minuit).
16 March	Death of Thomas MacGreevy.
June	*Eh Joe and Other Writings*, including *Act Without Words II* and *Film* (London: Faber).
July	*Come and Go*, English translation of *Va et vient* (London: Calder).
26 September	Directs first solo production, *Endspiel* (translation of *Endgame* by Elmar Tophoven) in Berlin.

(RTÉ, Channel 4, and Irish Film Board; DVD, London: Clarence Pictures).

2006

Samuel Beckett: Works for Radio: The Original Broadcasts: five works spanning the period 1957–1976 (CD, London: British Library Board).

Compiled by Cassandra Nelson

MS 2602

On. Say on. Be it said on, again on. Somehowon. Till no how on.

A place. Where none. For the body. To be in. Move in. Out
of. Back into. No. No out. In only. Stay in. On in. Nothing
more. Sweet blest all.

All ago, long ago. Nothing else ever. Ever tried. Ever failed.
No matter. Same again. Try again. Fail again. Fail better.

First the body. No. The place. No. Together. Either, now
the other. Sick of either try the other. Sick of it back sick
of the either. So on. Till sick of both. Throw up and go. Where
neither. Till sick of there. Throw up and back. A body again.
Where none. A place again. Where none. Fail again. Better again.
Or better worse. Fail worse again. Still worse again. Till sick
for good. Throw up for good. Go for good. Where neither for good.
Good and all.

It stands. What? Yes. up in the end and stand.
choice in the end but up and stand. Say the bones, Say for example the
bones. The say for example the earth, Ironhard. No mind and pain?
Say yes that the bones may pain till it must stand. Up somehow and
stand. Or a minimum. Say a minimum of mind where none to permit of
pain. Here of the bones they must up somehow and stand./Somehow
stand. Either. Providing pain. Here of bones. Other examples to come.
Of pain. Relief from. Change of.

All ago. But never so failed.
Worse failed. With care never worse failed.

Too much. light too much. Faint/light source unknown. Know
the minimum. Know nothing no. Not yet. At most the minimum. Meremost
minimum.

Long since it stood and No choice but stand. Up somehow and stand.
Somehow stand. That or shriek. The shriek so long on its way. No. No
shriek. Not yet. Simply pain. Simply up. Somehow the bones off the
ironhard. A time when how, now finally first if lying to begin it somehow
sits. Stage by stage. Then on from there. Stage by stage. Till finally
up. Not now. Fail better worse now.

Another. Head sunk on crippled hands. Vertex vertical. Eyes.
Seat of all.

No future in this. Alas yes.

It stands. See in the dim how at last it stands. In the
light source unknown. Before the downcast eyes. The staring
eyes. The eyes. staring eyes.

That shade. Lately lying. Long lying. Now standing. Somehow
standing. At long last. In the dim void. The body? Yes. That
the body. Say that the body. That shade the body. Somehow standing.
In the dim void.

A place. Where none. A time when try see Know. How small. How vast.
How if not boundless bounded. Whence the light. Not now. Know
better now. Unknow better now. Know only no out of. Into only. Hence
another place. Another place where none. Whither once whence no return.
No. Too much. No place but the one. None but the one where none. Whence
once in never out. Once somehow in. Beyondless. Thenceless there.
Thitherless there. Thitherless thenceless there.

Opening page of the first typescript of *Worstward Ho*, with
manuscript corrections
Courtesy of the Beckett International Foundation, University of Reading.
© The Estate of Samuel Beckett.

Company

A voice comes to one in the dark. Imagine.

To one on his back in the dark. This he can tell by the pressure on his hind parts and by how the dark changes when he shuts his eyes and again when he opens them again. Only a small part of what is said can be verified. As for example when he hears, You are on your back in the dark. Then he must acknowledge the truth of what is said. But by far the greater part of what is said cannot be verified. As for example when he hears, You first saw the light on such and such a day. Sometimes the two are combined as for example, You first saw the light on such and such a day and now you are on your back in the dark. A device perhaps from the incontrovertibility of the one to win credence for the other. That then is the proposition. To one on his back in the dark a voice tells of a past. With occasional allusion to a present and more rarely to a future as for example, You will end as you now are. And in another dark or in the same another devising it all for company. Quick leave him.

Use of the second person marks the voice. That of

3

the third that cankerous other. Could he speak to and of whom the voice speaks there would be a first. But he cannot. He shall not. You cannot. You shall not.

Apart from the voice and the faint sound of his breath there is no sound. None at least that he can hear. This he can tell by the faint sound of his breath.

Though now even less than ever given to wonder he cannot but sometimes wonder if it is indeed to and of him the voice is speaking. May not there be another with him in the dark to and of whom the voice is speaking? Is he not perhaps overhearing a communication not intended for him? If he is alone on his back in the dark why does the voice not say so? Why does it never say for example, You saw the light on such and such a day and now you are alone on your back in the dark? Why? Perhaps for no other reason than to kindle in his mind this faint uncertainty and embarrassment.

Your mind never active at any time is now even less than ever so. This is the type of assertion he does not question. You saw the light on such and such a day and your mind never active at any time is now even less than ever so. Yet a certain activity of mind however slight is a necessary complement of company.

That is why the voice does not say, You are on your back in the dark and have no mental activity of any kind. The voice alone is company but not enough. Its effect on the hearer is a necessary complement. Were it only to kindle in his mind the state of faint uncertainty and embarrassment mentioned above. But company apart this effect is clearly necessary. For were he merely to hear the voice and it to have no more effect on him than speech in Bantu or in Erse then might it not as well cease? Unless its object be by mere sound to plague one in need of silence. Or of course unless as above surmised directed at another.

A small boy you come out of Connolly's Stores holding your mother by the hand. You turn right and advance in silence southward along the highway. After some hundred paces you head inland and broach the long steep homeward. You make ground in silence hand in hand through the warm still summer air. It is late afternoon and after some hundred paces the sun appears above the crest of the rise. Looking up at the blue sky and then at your mother's face you break the silence asking her if it is not in reality much more distant than it appears. The sky that is. The blue sky. Receiving no answer you mentally reframe your question and some hundred paces later look up at her face again and ask her if it does not appear much less distant than in reality it is. For some reason you could never fathom this question must have angered her exceedingly. For she shook off your little hand and made you a cutting retort you have never forgotten.

If the voice is not speaking to him it must be speaking to another. So with what reason remains he reasons. To another of that other. Or of him. Or of another still. To another of that other or of him or of another still. To one on his back in the dark in any case. Of one on his back in the dark whether the same or another. So with what reason remains he reasons and reasons ill. For were the voice speaking not to him but to another then it must be of that other it is speaking and not of him or of another still. Since it speaks in the second person. Were it not of him to whom it is speaking speaking but of another it would not speak in the second person but in the third. For example, He first saw the light on such and such a day and now he is on his back in the dark. It is clear therefore that if it is not to him the voice is speaking but to another it is not of him either but of that other and none other to that other. So with what reason remains he reasons ill. In order to be company he must display a certain mental activity. But it need not be of a high order. Indeed it might be argued the lower the better. Up to a point. The lower the order of mental activity the better the company. Up to a point.

You first saw the light in the room you most likely were conceived in. The big bow window looked west to the mountain. Mainly west. For being bow it looked also a little south and a little north. Necessarily. A little south to more mountain and a little north to foothill and plain. The midwife was none other than a Dr. Hadden or Haddon. Straggling grey moustache and hunted look. It being a public holiday your father left the house soon after his breakfast with a flask and a package of his favourite egg sandwiches for a tramp in the mountains. There was nothing unusual in this. But on that particular morning his love of walking and wild scenery was not the only mover. But he was moved also to take himself off and out of the way by his aversion to the pains and general unpleasantness of labour and delivery. Hence the sandwiches which he relished at noon looking out to sea from the lee of a great rock on the first summit scaled. You may imagine his thoughts before and after as he strode through the gorse and heather. When he returned at nightfall he learned to his dismay from the maid at the back door that labour was still in swing. Despite its having begun before he left the house full ten hours earlier. He at once hastened to the coach-house some twenty yards distant where he housed his De Dion Bouton. He shut the doors behind him and climbed into the driver's seat. You may imagine his thoughts as he sat there in the dark not knowing what to think. Though footsore and weary he was on the point of setting out anew across the fields in the young moonlight when the maid came running to tell him it was over at last. Over!

You are an old man plodding along a narrow country road. You have been out since break of day and now it is evening. Sole sound in the silence your footfalls. Rather sole sounds for they vary from one to the next. You listen to each one and add it in your mind to the growing sum of those that went before. You halt with bowed head on the verge of the ditch and convert into yards. On the basis now of two steps per yard. So many since dawn to add to yesterday's. To yesteryear's. To yesteryears'. Days other than today and so akin. The giant tot in miles. In leagues. How often round the earth already. Halted too at your elbow during these computations your father's shade. In his old tramping rags. Finally on side by side from nought anew.

The voice comes to him now from one quarter and

now from another. Now faint from afar and now a murmur in his ear. In the course of a single sentence it may change place and tone. Thus for example clear from above his upturned face, You first saw the light at Easter and now. Then a murmur in his ear, You are on your back in the dark. Or of course vice versa. Another trait its long silences when he dare almost hope it is at an end. Thus to take the same example clear from above his upturned face, You first saw the light of day the day Christ died and now. Then long after on his nascent hope the murmur, You are on your back in the dark. Or of course vice versa.

Another trait its repetitiousness. Repeatedly with only minor variants the same bygone. As if willing him by this dint to make it his. To confess, Yes I remember. Perhaps even to have a voice. To murmur, Yes I remember. What an addition to company that would be! A voice in the first person singular. Murmuring now and then, Yes I remember.

An old beggar woman is fumbling at a big garden gate. Half blind. You know the place well. Stone deaf and not in her right mind the woman of the house is a crony of your mother. She was sure she could fly once in the air. So one day she launched herself from a first-floor window. On the way home from

9

kindergarten on your tiny cycle you see the poor old beggar woman trying to get in. You dismount and open the gate for her. She blesses you. What were her words? God reward you little master. Some such words. God save you little master.

A faint voice at loudest. It slowly ebbs till almost out of hearing. Then slowly back to faint full. At each slow ebb hope slowly dawns that it is dying. He must know it will flow again. And yet at each slow ebb hope slowly dawns that it is dying.

Slowly he entered dark and silence and lay there for so long that with what judgement remained he judged them to be final. Till one day the voice. One day! Till in the end the voice saying, You are on your back in the dark. Those its first words. Long pause for him to believe his ears and then from another quarter the same. Next the vow not to cease till hearing cease. You are on your back in the dark and not till hearing cease will this voice cease. Or another way. As in shadow he lay and only the odd sound slowly silence fell and darkness gathered. That were perhaps better company. For what odd sound? Whence the shadowy light?

You stand at the tip of the high board. High above

the sea. In it your father's upturned face. Upturned to you. You look down to the loved trusted face. He calls to you to jump. He calls, Be a brave boy. The red round face. The thick moustache. The greying hair. The swell sways it under and sways it up again. The far call again, Be a brave boy. Many eyes upon you. From the water and from the bathing place.

The odd sound. What a mercy to have that to turn to. Now and then. In dark and silence to close as if to light the eyes and hear a sound. Some object moving from its place to its last place. Some soft thing softly stirring soon to stir no more. To darkness visible to close the eyes and hear if only that. Some soft thing softly stirring soon to stir no more.

By the voice a faint light is shed. Dark lightens while it sounds. Deepens when it ebbs. Lightens with flow back to faint full. Is whole again when it ceases. You are on your back in the dark. Had the eyes been open then they would have marked a change.

Whence the shadowy light? What company in the dark! To close the eyes and try to imagine that. Whence once the shadowy light. No source. As if faintly luminous all his little void. What can he have seen then above his upturned face. To close the eyes in the dark and try to imagine that.

Another trait the flat tone. No life. Same flat tone at all times. For its affirmations. For its negations. For its interrogations. For its exclamations. For its imperations. Same flat tone. You were once. You were never. Were you ever? Oh never to have been! Be again. Same flat tone.

Can he move? Does he move? Should he move? What a help that would be. When the voice fails. Some movement however small. Were it but of a hand closing. Or opening if closed to begin. What a help that would be in the dark! To close the eyes and see that hand. Palm upward filling the whole field. The lines. The fingers slowly down. Or up if down to begin. The lines of that old palm.

There is of course the eye. Filling the whole field. The hood slowly down. Or up if down to begin. The globe. All pupil. Staring up. Hooded. Bared. Hooded again. Bared again.

If he were to utter after all? However feebly. What an addition to company that would be! You are on your back in the dark and one day you will utter again. One day! In the end. In the end you will utter again. Yes I remember. That was I. That was I then.

You are alone in the garden. Your mother is in the kitchen making ready for afternoon tea with Mrs. Coote. Making the wafer-thin bread and butter. From behind a bush you watch Mrs. Coote arrive. A small thin sour woman. Your mother answers her saying, He is playing in the garden. You climb to near the top of a great fir. You sit a little listening to all the sounds. Then throw yourself off. The great boughs break your fall. The needles. You lie a little with your face to the ground. Then climb the tree again. Your mother answers Mrs. Coote again saying, He has been a very naughty boy.

What with what feeling remains does he feel about now as compared to then? When with what judgement remained he judged his condition final. As well inquire what he felt then about then as compared to before. When he still moved or tarried in remains of light. As then there was no then so there is none now.

In another dark or in the same another devising it all for company. This at first sight seems clear. But as the eye dwells it grows obscure. Indeed the longer the

eye dwells the obscurer it grows. Till the eye closes
and freed from pore the mind inquires, What does
this mean? What finally does this mean that at first
sight seemed clear? Till it the mind too closes as it
were. As the window might close of a dark empty
room. The single window giving on outer dark. Then
nothing more. No. Unhappily no. Pangs of faint light
and stirrings still. Unformulable gropings of the
mind. Unstillable.

Nowhere in particular on the way from A to Z. Or
say for verisimilitude the Ballyogan Road. That dear
old back road. Somewhere on the Ballyogan Road
in lieu of nowhere in particular. Where no truck
any more. Somewhere on the Ballyogan Road on the
way from A to Z. Head sunk totting up the tally
on the verge of the ditch. Foothills to left. Croker's
Acres ahead. Father's shade to right and a little to the
rear. So many times already round the earth. Topcoat
once green stiff with age and grime from chin to
insteps. Battered once buff block hat and quarterboots still a match. No other garments if any to be
seen. Out since break of day and night now falling.
Reckoning ended on together from nought anew. As
if bound for Stepaside. When suddenly you cut
through the hedge and vanish hobbling east across
the gallops.

For why or? Why in another dark or in the same? And whose voice asking this? Who asks, Whose voice asking this? And answers, His soever who devises it all. In the same dark as his creature or in another. For company. Who asks in the end, Who asks? And in the end answers as above? And adds long after to himself, Unless another still. Nowhere to be found. Nowhere to be sought. The unthinkable last of all. Unnamable. Last person. I. Quick leave him.

The light there was then. On your back in the dark the light there was then. Sunless cloudless brightness. You slip away at break of day and climb to your hiding place on the hillside. A nook in the gorse. East beyond the sea the faint shape of high mountain. Seventy miles away according to your Longman. For the third or fourth time in your life. The first time you told them and were derided. All you had seen was cloud. So now you hoard it in your heart with the rest. Back home at nightfall supperless to bed. You lie in the dark and are back in that light. Straining out from your nest in the gorse with your eyes across the water till they ache. You close them while you count a hundred. Then open and strain again. Again and again. Till in the end it is there. Palest blue against the pale sky. You lie in the dark and are back in that light. Fall asleep in that sunless cloudless light. Sleep till morning light.

Deviser of the voice and of its hearer and of himself. Deviser of himself for company. Leave it at that. He speaks of himself as of another. He says speaking of himself, He speaks of himself as of another. Himself he devises too for company. Leave it at that. Confusion too is company up to a point. Better hope deferred than none. Up to a point. Till the heart starts to sicken. Company too up to a point. Better a sick heart than none. Till it starts to break. So speaking of himself he concludes for the time being, For the time being leave it at that.

In the same dark as his creature or in another not yet imagined. Nor in what position. Whether standing or sitting or lying or in some other position in the dark. These are among the matters yet to be imagined. Matters of which as yet no inkling. The test is company. Which of the two darks is the better company. Which of all imaginable positions has the most to offer in the way of company. And similarly for the other matters yet to be imagined. Such as if such decisions irreversible. Let him for example after due imagination decide in favour of the supine position or prone and this in practice prove less companionable than anticipated. May he then or may he not replace it by another? Such as huddled with his legs drawn up within the semicircle of his arms and his head on his knees. Or in motion. Crawling on all fours. Another in another dark or in the same crawling on all fours devising it all for company. Or some other form of motion. The possible encounters. A dead rat. What an addition to company that would be! A rat long dead.

Might not the hearer be improved? Made more companionable if not downright human. Mentally perhaps there is room for enlivenment. An attempt at reflexion at least. At recall. At speech even. Conation of some kind however feeble. A trace of emotion. Signs of distress. A sense of failure. Without loss of character. Delicate ground. But physically? Must he lie inert to the end? Only the eyelids stirring on and off since technically they must. To let in and shut out the dark. Might he not cross his feet? On and off. Now left on right and now a little later the reverse. No. Quite out of keeping. He lie with crossed feet? One glance dispels. Some movement of the hands? A hand. A clenching and unclenching. Difficult to justify. Or raised to brush away a fly. But there are no flies. Then why not let there be? The temptation is great. Let there be a fly. For him to brush away. A live fly mistaking him for dead. Made aware of its error and renewing it incontinent. What an addition to company that would be! A live fly mistaking him for dead. But no. He would not brush away a fly.

You take pity on a hedgehog out in the cold and put it in an old hatbox with some worms. This box with the hog inside you then place in a disused hutch wedging the door open for the poor creature to come and go at will. To go in search of food and having eaten to regain the warmth and security of its box in the hutch. There then is the hedgehog in its box in the hutch with enough worms to tide it over. A last look to make sure all is as it should be before taking yourself off to look for something else to pass the time heavy already on your hands at that tender age. The glow at your good deed is slower than usual to cool and fade. You glowed readily in those days but seldom for long. Hardly had the glow been kindled by some good deed on your part or by some little triumph over your rivals or by a word of praise from your parents or mentors when it would begin to cool and fade leaving you in a very short time as chill and dim as before. Even in those days. But not this day. It was on an autumn afternoon you found the hedgehog and took pity on it in the way described and you were still the better for it when your bedtime came.

Kneeling at your bedside you included it the hedge-hog in your detailed prayer to God to bless all you loved. And tossing in your warm bed waiting for sleep to come you were still faintly glowing at the thought of what a fortunate hedgehog it was to have crossed your path as it did. A narrow clay path edged with sere box edging. As you stood there wondering how best to pass the time till bedtime it parted the edging on the one side and was making straight for the edging on the other when you entered its life. Now the next morning not only was the glow spent but a great uneasiness had taken its place. A suspicion that all was perhaps not as it should be. That rather than do as you did you had perhaps better let good alone and the hedgehog pursue its way. Days if not weeks passed before you could bring yourself to return to the hutch. You have never forgotten what you found then. You are on your back in the dark and have never forgotten what you found then. The mush. The stench.

Impending for some time the following. Need for company not continuous. Moments when his own unrelieved a relief. Intrusion of voice at such. Similarly image of hearer. Similarly his own. Regret then at having brought them about and problem how dispel them. Finally what meant by his own unrelieved? What possible relief? Leave it at that for the moment.

Let the hearer be named H. Aspirate. Haitch. You Haitch are on your back in the dark. And let him know his name. No longer any question of his over-hearing. Of his not being meant. Though logically none in any case. Of words murmured in his ear to wonder if to him! So he is. So that faint uneasiness lost. That faint hope. To one with so few occasions to feel. So inapt to feel. Asking nothing better in so far as he can ask anything than to feel nothing. Is it desirable? No. Would he gain thereby in companion-ability? No. Then let him not be named H. Let him be again as he was. The hearer. Unnamable. You.

Imagine closer the place where he lies. Within rea-son. To its form and dimensions a clue is given by the voice afar. Receding afar or there with abrupt salta-tion or resuming there after pause. From above and from all sides and levels with equal remoteness at its most remote. At no time from below. So far. Suggesting one lying on the floor of a hemispherical chamber of generous diameter with ear dead centre. How generous? Given faintness of voice at its least faint some sixty feet should suffice or thirty from ear to any given point of encompassing surface. So much for form and dimensions. And composition? What and where clue to that if any anywhere. Reserve for the moment. Basalt is tempting. Black basalt. But reserve for the moment. So he imagines to himself as voice and hearer pall. But further imagination shows him to have imagined ill. For with what right affirm of a faint sound that it is a less faint made fainter by farness and not a true faint near at hand? Or of a faint fading to fainter that it recedes and not in situ decreases. If with none then no light from the voice on the place where our old hearer lies. In immeasurable dark. Contourless. Leave it at that for the moment. Adding only, What kind of imagination is this so reason-ridden? A kind of its own.

Another devising it all for company. In the same dark as his creature or in another. Quick imagine. The same.

Might not the voice be improved? Made more companionable. Say changing now for some time past though no tense in the dark in that dim mind. All at once over and in train and to come. But for the other say for some time past some improvement. Same flat tone as initially imagined and same repetitiousness. No improving those. But less mobility. Less variety of faintness. As if seeking optimum position.

From which to discharge with greatest effect. The ideal amplitude for effortless audition. Neither offending the ear with loudness nor through converse excess constraining it to strain. How far more companionable such an organ than it initially in haste imagined. How far more likely to achieve its object. To have the hearer have a past and acknowledge it. You were born on an Easter Friday after long labour. Yes I remember. The sun had not long sunk behind the larches. Yes I remember. As best to erode the drop must strike unwavering. Upon the place beneath.

The last time you went out the snow lay on the ground. You now on your back in the dark stand that morning on the sill having pulled the door gently to behind you. You lean back against the door with bowed head making ready to set out. By the time you open your eyes your feet have disappeared and the skirts of your greatcoat come to rest on the surface of the snow. The dark scene seems lit from below. You see yourself at that last outset leaning against the door with closed eyes waiting for the word from you to go. To be gone. Then the snowlit scene. You lie in the dark with closed eyes and see yourself there as described making ready to strike out and away across the expanse of light. You hear again the click of the door pulled gently to and the silence before the steps can start. Next thing you are on your way across the white pasture afrolic with lambs in spring and strewn with red placentae. You take the course you always take which is a beeline for the gap or ragged point in the quickset that forms the western fringe. Thither from your entering the pasture you need normally from eighteen hundred to two thousand paces depending on your humour and the state of the ground. But on this last morning many more will be required. Many many more. The beeline is so familiar to your feet that if necessary they could keep to it and you sightless with error on arrival of not more than a few feet north or south. And indeed without any such necessity unless from within this is what they normally do and not only here. For you advance if not with closed eyes though this as often as not at least with them fixed on the momentary ground before your feet. That is all of nature you have seen. Since finally you bowed your head. The fleeting ground before your feet. From time to time. You do not count your steps any more. For the simple reason they number each day the same. Average day in day out the same. The way being always the same. You keep count of the days and every tenth day multiply. And add. Your father's shade is not with you any more. It fell out long ago. You do not hear your footfalls any more. Unhearing unseeing you go your way.

Day after day. The same way. As if there were no other any more. For you there is no other any more. You used never to halt except to make your reckoning. So as to plod on from nought anew. This need removed as we have seen there is none in theory to halt any more. Save perhaps a moment at the outermost point. To gather yourself together for the return. And yet you do. As never before. Not for tiredness. You are no more tired now than you always were. Not because of age. You are no older now than you always were. And yet you halt as never before. So that the same hundred yards you used to cover in a matter of three to four minutes may now take you anything from fifteen to twenty. The foot falls unbidden in midstep or next for lift cleaves to the ground bringing the body to a stand. Then a speechlessness whereof the gist, Can they go on? Or better, Shall they go on? The barest gist. Stilled when finally as always hitherto they do. You lie in the dark with closed eyes and see the scene. As you could not at the time. The dark cope of sky. The dazzling land. You at a standstill in the midst. The quarterboots sunk to the tops. The skirts of the greatcoat resting on the snow. In the old bowed head in the old block hat speechless misgiving. Halfway across the pasture on your beeline to the gap. The unerring feet fast. You look behind you as you could not then and see their trail. A great swerve. Withershins. Almost as if all at once the heart too heavy. In the end too heavy.

Bloom of adulthood. Imagine a whiff of that. On your back in the dark you remember. Ah you you remember. Cloudless May day. She joins you in the little summerhouse. A rustic hexahedron. Entirely of logs. Both larch and fir. Six feet across. Eight from floor to vertex. Area twenty-four square feet to furthest decimal. Two small multicoloured lights vis-à-vis. Small stained diamond panes. Under each a ledge. There on summer Sundays after his midday meal your father loved to retreat with *Punch* and a cushion. The waist of his trousers unbuttoned he sat on the one ledge turning the pages. You on the other with your feet dangling. When he chuckled you tried to chuckle too. When his chuckle died yours too. That you should try to imitate his chuckle pleased and tickled him greatly and sometimes he would chuckle for no other reason than to hear you try to chuckle too. Sometimes you turn your head and look out through a rose-red pane. You press your little nose against the pane and all without is rosy. The years have flown and there at the same place as then you sit in the bloom of adulthood bathed in rainbow light gazing before you. She is late. You close your eyes and try to calculate the volume. Simple sums you find a

help in times of trouble. A haven. You arrive in the
end at seven cubic yards approximately. Even still in
the timeless dark you find figures a comfort. You
assume a certain heart rate and reckon how many
thumps a day. A week. A month. A year. And assuming a certain lifetime a lifetime. Till the last thump.
But for the moment with hardly more than seventy
American billion behind you you sit in the little summerhouse working out the volume. Seven cubic yards
approximately. This strikes you for some reason as
improbable and you set about your sum anew. But
you have not made much headway when her light
step is heard. Light for a woman of her size. You open
with quickening pulse your eyes and a moment later
that seems an eternity her face appears at the window. Mainly blue in this position the natural pallor
you so admire as indeed from it no doubt wholly blue
your own. For natural pallor is a property you have in
common. The violet lips do not return your smile.
Now this window being flush with your eyes from
where you sit and the floor as near as no matter with
the outer ground you cannot but wonder if she has
not sunk to her knees. Knowing from experience that
the height or length you have in common is the sum
of equal segments. For when bolt upright or lying at
full stretch you cleave face to face then your knees
meet and your pubes and the hairs of your heads

mingle. Does it follow from this that the loss of height for the body that sits is the same as for it that kneels? At this point assuming height of seat adjustable as in the case of certain piano stools you close your eyes the better with mental measure to measure and compare the first and second segments namely from sole to knee-pad and thence to pelvic girdle. How given you were both moving and at rest to the closed eye in your waking hours! By day and by night. To that perfect dark. That shadowless light. Simply to be gone. Or for affair as now. A single leg appears. Seen from above. You separate the segments and lay them side by side. It is as you half surmised. The upper is the longer and the sitter's loss the greater when seat at knee level. You leave the pieces lying there and open your eyes to find her sitting before you. All dead still. The ruby lips do not return your smile. Your gaze descends to the breasts. You do not remember them so big. To the abdomen. Same impression. Dissolve to your father's straining against the unbuttoned waistband. Can it be she is with child without your having asked for as much as her hand? You go back into your mind. She too did you but know it has closed her eyes. So you sit face to face in the little summerhouse. With eyes closed and your hands on your pubes. In that rainbow light. That dead still.

Wearied by such stretch of imagining he ceases and all ceases. Till feeling the need for company again he tells himself to call the hearer M at least. For readier reference. Himself some other character. W. Devising it all himself included for company. In the same dark as M when last heard of. In what posture and whether fixed or mobile left open. He says further to himself referring to himself, When last he referred to himself it was to say he was in the same dark as his creature. Not in another as once seemed possible. The same. As more companionable. And that his posture there remained to be devised. And to be decided whether fast or mobile. Which of all imaginable postures least liable to pall? Which of motion or of rest the more entertaining in the long run? And in the same breath too soon to say and why after all not say without further ado what can later be unsaid and what if it could not? What then? Could he now if he chose move out of the dark he chose when last heard of and away from his creature into another? Should he now decide to lie and come later to regret it could he then rise to his feet for example and lean against a wall or pace to and fro? Could M be reimagined in an easy chair? With hands free to go to his assistance? There in the same dark as his creature he leaves himself to these perplexities while wondering as every now and then he wonders in the back of his mind if the woes of the world are all they used to be. In his day.

M so far as follows. On his back in a dark place form and dimensions yet to be devised. Hearing on and off a voice of which uncertain whether addressed to him or to another sharing his situation. There being nothing to show when it describes correctly his situation that the description is not for the benefit of another in the same situation. Vague distress at the vague thought of his perhaps overhearing a confidence when he hears for example, You are on your back in the dark. Doubts gradually dashed as voice from questing far and wide closes in upon him. When it ceases no other sound than his breath. When it ceases long enough vague hope it may have said its last. Mental activity of a low order. Rare flickers of reasoning of no avail. Hope and despair and suchlike barely felt. How current situation arrived at unclear. No that then to compare to this now. Only eyelids move. When for relief from outer and inner dark they close and open respectively. Other small local movements eventually within moderation not to be despaired of. But no improvement by means of such achieved so far. Or on a higher plane by such addition to company as a movement of sustained sorrow or desire or remorse or curiosity or anger and so on.

Or by some successful act of intellection as were he to think to himself referring to himself, Since he cannot think he will give up trying. Is there anything to add to this esquisse? His unnamability. Even M must go. So W reminds himself of his creature as so far created. W? But W too is creature. Figment.

Yet another then. Of whom nothing. Devising figments to temper his nothingness. Quick leave him. Pause and again in panic to himself, Quick leave him.

Devised deviser devising it all for company. In the same figment dark as his figments. In what posture and if or not as hearer in his for good not yet devised. Is not one immovable enough? Why duplicate this particular solace? Then let him move. Within reason. On all fours. A moderate crawl torso well clear of the ground eyes front alert. If this no better than nothing cancel. If possible. And in the void regained another motion. Or none. Leaving only the most helpful posture to be devised. But to be going on with let him crawl. Crawl and fall. Crawl again and fall again. In the same figment dark as his other figments.

From ranging far and wide as if in quest the voice comes to rest and constant faintness. To rest where? Imagine warily.

Above the upturned face. Falling tangent to the crown. So that in the faint light it sheds were there a mouth to be seen he would not see it. Roll as he might his eyes. Height from the ground?

Arm's length. Force? Low. A mother's stooping over cradle from behind. She moves aside to let the father look. In his turn he murmurs to the newborn. Flat tone unchanged. No trace of love.

You are on your back at the foot of an aspen. In its trembling shade. She at right angles propped on her elbows head between her hands. Your eyes opened and closed have looked in hers looking in yours. In your dark you look in them again. Still. You feel on your face the fringe of her long black hair stirring in the still air. Within the tent of hair your faces are hidden from view. She murmurs, Listen to the leaves. Eyes in each other's eyes you listen to the leaves. In their trembling shade.

Crawling and falling then. Crawling again and falling again. If this finally no improvement on nothing he can always fall for good. Or have never risen to his knees. Contrive how such crawl unlike the voice may serve to chart the area. However roughly. First what is the unit of crawl? Corresponding to the footstep of erect locomotion. He rises to all fours and makes ready to set out. Hands and knees angles of an oblong two foot long width irrelevant. Finally say left knee moves forward six inches thus half halving distance between it and homologous hand. Which then in due course in its turn moves forward by as much. Oblong now rhomboid. But for no longer than it takes right knee and hand to follow suit. Oblong restored. So on till he drops. Of all modes of crawl this the repent amble is possibly the least common. And so possibly of all the most diverting.

So as he crawls the mute count. Grain by grain in the mind. One two three four one. Knee hand knee hand two. One foot. Till say after five he falls. Then sooner or later on from nought anew. One two three four one. Knee hand knee hand two. Six. So on. In what he wills a beeline. Till having encountered no obstacle discouraged he heads back the way he came. From nought anew. Or in some quite different direction. In what he hopes a beeline. Till again with no dead end for his pains he renounces and embarks on yet another course. From nought anew. Well aware or little doubting how darkness may deflect. Withershins on account of the heart. Or conversely to shortest path convert deliberate veer. Be that as it may and crawl as he will no bourne as yet. As yet imaginable. Hand knee hand knee as he will. Bourneless dark.

Would it be reasonable to imagine the hearer as mentally quite inert? Except when he hears. That is when the voice sounds. For what if not it and his breath is there for him to hear? Aha! The crawl. Does he hear the crawl? The fall? What an addition to company were he but to hear the crawl. The fall. The rising to all fours again. The crawl resumed. And wonder to himself what in the world such sounds might signify. Reserve for a duller moment. What if not sound could set his mind in motion? Sight? The temptation is strong to decree there is nothing to see. But too late for the moment. For he sees a change of dark when he opens or shuts his eyes. And he may see the faint light the voice imagined to shed. Rashly imagined. Light infinitely faint it is true since now no more than a mere murmur. Here suddenly seen how his eyes close as soon as the voice sounds. Should they happen to be open at the time. So light as let be faintest light no longer perceived than the time it takes the lid to fall. Taste? The taste in his mouth? Long since dulled. Touch? The thrust of the ground against his bones. All the way from calcaneum to bump of philoprogenitiveness. Might not a notion to stir ruffle his apathy? To turn on his side. On his face.

For a change. Let that much of want be conceded. With attendant relief that the days are no more when he could writhe in vain. Smell? His own? Long since dulled. And a barrier to others if any. Such as might have once emitted a rat long dead. Or some other carrion. Yet to be imagined. Unless the crawler smell. Aha! The crawling creator. Might the crawling creator be reasonably imagined to smell? Even fouler than his creature. Stirring now and then to wonder that mind so lost to wonder. To wonder what in the world can be making that alien smell. Whence in the world those wafts of villainous smell. How much more companionable could his creator but smell. Could he but smell his creator. Some sixth sense? Inexplicable premonition of impending ill? Yes or no? No. Pure reason? Beyond experience. God is love. Yes or no? No.

Can the crawling creator crawling in the same create dark as his creature create while crawling? One of the questions he put to himself as between two crawls he lay. And if the obvious answer were not far to seek the most helpful was another matter. And many crawls were necessary and the like number of prostrations before he could finally make up his imagination on this score. Adding to himself without conviction in the same breath as always that no answer of his was sacred. Come what might the answer he hazarded in the end was no he could not. Crawling in the dark in the way described was too serious a matter and too all-engrossing to permit of any other business were it only the conjuring of something out of nothing. For he had not only as perhaps too hastily imagined to cover the ground in this special way but rectigrade into the bargain to the best of his ability. And furthermore to count as he went adding half foot to half foot and retain in his memory the ever-changing sum of those gone before. And finally to maintain eyes and ears at a high level of alertness for any clue however small to the nature of the place to which imagination perhaps unadvisedly had consigned him. So while in the same breath deploring a fancy so reason-ridden and observing how revocable its flights he could not but answer finally no he could not. Could not conceivably create while crawling in the same create dark as his creature.

A strand. Evening. Light dying. Soon none left to die. No. No such thing then as no light. Died on to dawn and never died. You stand with your back to the wash. No sound but its. Ever fainter as it slowly ebbs. Till it slowly flows again. You lean on a long staff. Your hands rest on the knob and on them your head. Were your eyes to open they would first see far below in the last rays the skirt of your greatcoat and the uppers of your boots emerging from the sand. Then and it alone till it vanishes the shadow of the staff on the sand. Vanishes from your sight. Moonless starless night. Were your eyes to open dark would lighten.

Crawls and falls. Lies. Lies in the dark with closed eyes resting from his crawl. Recovering. Physically and from his disappointment at having crawled again in vain. Perhaps saying to himself, Why crawl at all? Why not just lie in the dark with closed eyes and give up? Give up all. Have done with all. With bootless crawl and figments comfortless. But if on occasion so disheartened it is seldom for long. For little by little as he lies the craving for company revives. In which to escape from his own. The need to hear that voice again. If only saying again, You are on your back in the dark. Or if only, You first saw the light and cried at the close of the day when in darkness Christ at the ninth hour cried and died. The need eyes closed the better to hear to see that glimmer shed. Or with adjunction of some human weakness to improve the hearer. For example an itch beyond reach of the hand or better still within while the hand immovable. An unscratchable itch. What an addition to company that would be! Or last if not least resort to ask himself what precisely he means when he speaks of himself loosely as lying. Which in other words of all the innumerable ways of lying is likely to prove in the long run the most endearing. If having crawled in the way described he falls it would normally be on his face. Indeed given the degree of his fatigue and discouragement at this point it is hard to see how he could do otherwise. But once fallen and lying on his face there is no reason why he should not turn over on one or other of his sides or on his only back and so lie should any of these three postures offer better company than any of the other three. The supine though most tempting he must finally disallow as being already supplied by the hearer. With regard to the sidelong one glance is enough to dispel them both. Leaving him with no other choice than the prone. But how prone? Prone how? How disposed the legs? The arms? The head? Prone in the dark he strains to see how best he may lie prone. How most companionably.

See hearer clearer. Which of all the ways of lying supine the least likely in the long run to pall? After long straining eyes closed prone in the dark the following. But first naked or covered? If only with a sheet. Naked. Ghostly in the voice's glimmer that bonewhite flesh for company. Head resting mainly on occipital bump aforesaid. Legs joined at attention. Feet splayed ninety degrees. Hands invisibly manacled crossed on pubis. Other details as need felt. Leave him at that for the moment.

Numb with the woes of your kind you raise none the less your head from off your hands and open your eyes. You turn on without moving from your place the light above you. Your eyes light on the watch lying beneath it. But instead of reading the hour of night they follow round and round the second hand now followed and now preceded by its shadow. Hours later it seems to you as follows. At 60 seconds and 30 seconds shadow hidden by hand. From 60 to 30 shadow precedes hand at a distance increasing from zero at 60 to maximum at 15 and thence decreasing to new zero at 30. From 30 to 60 shadow follows hand at a distance increasing from zero at 30 to maximum at 45 and thence decreasing to new zero at 60. Slant light now to dial by moving either to either side and hand hides shadow at two quite different points as for example 50 and 20. Indeed at any two quite different points whatever depending on degree of slant. But however great or small the slant and more or less remote from initial 60 and 30 the new points of zero shadow the space between the two remains one of 30 seconds. The shadow emerges from under hand at any point whatever of its circuit to follow or precede it for the space of 30 seconds. Then disappears infinitely briefly before emerging again to precede or follow it for the space of 30 seconds again. And so on and on. This would seem to be the one constant. For the very distance itself between hand and shadow varies as the degree of slant. But however great or small this distance it invariably waxes and wanes from nothing to a maximum 15 seconds later and to nothing again 15 seconds later again respectively. And so on and on. This would seem to be a second constant. More might have been observed on the subject of this second hand and its shadow in their seemingly endless parallel rotation round and round the dial and other variables and constants brought to light and errors if any corrected in what had seemed so far. But unable to continue you bow your head back to where it was and with closed eyes return to the woes of your kind. Dawn finds you still in this position. The low sun shines on you through the eastern window and flings all along the floor your shadow and that of the lamp left lit above you. And those of other objects also.

What visions in the dark of light! Who exclaims

thus? Who asks who exclaims, What visions in the shadeless dark of light and shade! Yet another still? Devising it all for company. What a further addition to company that would be! Yet another still devising it all for company. Quick leave him.

Somehow at any price to make an end when you could go out no more you sat huddled in the dark. Having covered in your day some twenty-five thousand leagues or roughly thrice the girdle. And never once overstepped a radius of one from home. Home! So sat waiting to be purged the old lutist cause of Dante's first quarter-smile and now perhaps singing praises with some section of the blest at last. To whom here in any case farewell. The place is windowless. When as you sometimes do to void the fluid you open your eyes dark lessens. Thus you now on your back in the dark once sat huddled there your body having shown you it could go out no more. Out no more to walk the little winding back roads and interjacent pastures now alive with flocks and now deserted. With at your elbow for long years your father's shade in his old tramping rags and then for long years alone. Adding step after step to the ever mounting sum of those already accomplished. Halting now and then with bowed head to fix the score. Then on from nought anew. Huddled thus you find yourself imagining you are not alone while knowing full well that nothing has occurred to make this possible. The process continues none the less lapped as it were in its meaninglessness. You do not murmur in so many words, I know this doomed to fail and yet persist. No. For the first personal singular and a fortiori plural pronoun had never any place in your vocabulary. But without a word you view yourself to this effect as you would a stranger suffering say from Hodgkin's disease or if you prefer Percival Pott's surprised at prayer. From time to time with unexpected grace you lie. Simultaneously the various parts set out. The arms unclasp the knees. The head lifts. The legs start to straighten. The trunk tilts backward. And together these and countless others continue on their respective ways till they can go no further and together come to rest. Supine now you resume your fable where the act of lying cut it short. And persist till the converse operation cuts it short again. So in the dark now huddled and now supine you toil in vain. And just as from the former position to the latter the shift grows easier in time and more alacrious so from the latter to the former the reverse is true. Till from the occasional relief it was supineness becomes habitual and finally the rule. You now on your back in the dark shall not rise again to clasp your legs in your arms and bow down your head till it can bow down no further. But with face upturned for good labour in vain at your fable. Till finally you hear how words are coming to an end. With every inane word a little nearer to the last. And how the fable too. The fable of one with you in the dark. The fable of one fabling of one with you in the dark. And how better in the end labour lost and silence. And you as you always were.

Alone.

Ill Seen Ill Said

From where she lies she sees Venus rise. On. From where she lies when the skies are clear she sees Venus rise followed by the sun. Then she rails at the source of all life. On. At evening when the skies are clear she savours its star's revenge. At the other window. Rigid upright on her old chair she watches for the radiant one. Her old deal spindlebacked kitchen chair. It emerges from out the last rays and sinking ever brighter is engulfed in its turn. On. She sits on erect and rigid in the deepening gloom. Such helplessness to move she cannot help. Heading on foot for a particular point often she freezes on the way. Unable till long after to move on not knowing whither or for what purpose. Down on her knees especially she finds it hard not to remain so forever. Hand resting on hand on some convenient support. Such as the foot of her bed. And on them her head. There then she sits as though turned to stone face to the night. Save for the white of her hair and faintly bluish white of face and hands all is black. For an eye having no need of light to see. All this in the present as had she the misfortune to be still of this world.

The cabin. Its situation. Careful. On. At the

45

inexistent centre of a formless place. Rather more circular than otherwise finally. Flat to be sure. To cross it in a straight line takes her from five to ten minutes. Depending on her speed and radius taken. Here she who loves to – here she who now can only stray never strays. Stones increasingly abound. Ever scanter even the rankest weed. Meagre pastures hem it round on which it slowly gains. With none to gainsay. To have gainsaid. As if doomed to spread. How come a cabin in such a place? How came? Careful. Before replying that in the far past at the time of its building there was clover growing to its very walls. Implying furthermore that it the culprit. And from it as from an evil core that the what is the wrong word the evil spread. And none to urge – none to have urged its demolition. As if doomed to endure. Question answered. Chalkstones of striking effect in the light of the moon. Let it be in opposition when the skies are clear. Quick then still under the spell of Venus quick to the other window to see the other marvel rise. How whiter and whiter as it climbs it whitens more and more the stones. Rigid with face and hands against the pane she stands and marvels long.

The two zones form a roughly circular whole. As though outlined by a trembling hand. Diameter. Careful. Say one furlong. On an average. Beyond the unknown. Mercifully. The feeling at times of being below sea level. Especially at night when the skies are clear. Invisible nearby sea. Inaudible. The entire surface under grass. Once clear of the zone of stones. Save where it has receded from the chalky soil. Innumerable white scabs all shapes and sizes. Of striking effect in the light of the moon. In the way of animals ovines only. After long hesitation. They are white and make do with little. Whence suddenly come no knowing nor whither as suddenly gone. Unshepherded they stray as they list. Flowers? Careful. Alone the odd crocus still at lambing time. And man? Shut of at last? Alas no. For will she not be surprised one day to find him gone? Surprised no she is beyond surprise. How many? A figure come what may. Twelve. Wherewith to furnish the horizon's narrow round. She raises her eyes and sees one. Turns away and sees another. So on. Always afar. Still or receding. She never once saw one come toward her. Or she forgets. She forgets. Are they always the same? Do they see her? Enough.

A moor would have better met the case. Were there a case better to meet. There had to be lambs. Rightly or wrongly. A moor would have allowed of them. Lambs for their whiteness. And for other reasons as yet obscure. Another reason. And so that there may be none. At lambing time. That from one moment to the next she may raise her eyes to find them gone. A moor would have allowed of them. In any case too late. And what lambs. No trace of frolic. White splotches in the grass. Aloof from the unheeding ewes. Still. Then a moment straying. Then still again. To think there is still life in this age. Gently gently.

She is drawn to a certain spot. At times. There stands a stone. It it is draws her. Rounded rectangular block three times as high as wide. Four. Her stature now. Her lowly stature. When it draws she must to it. She cannot see it from her door. Blindfold she could find her way. With herself she has no more converse. Never had much. Now none. As had she the misfortune to be still of this world. But when the stone draws then to her feet the prayer, Take her. Especially at night when the skies are clear. With moon or without. They take her and halt her before it. There she too as if of stone. But black. Sometimes in the light of the moon. Mostly of the stars alone. Does she envy it?

To the imaginary stranger the dwelling appears deserted. Under constant watch it betrays no sign of life. The eye glued to one or the other window has nothing but black drapes for its pains. Motionless against the door he listens long. No sound. Knocks. No answer. Watches all night in vain for the least glimmer. Returns at last to his own and avows, No one. She shows herself only to her own. But she has no own. Yes yes she has one. And who has her.

There was a time when she did not appear in the zone of stones. A long time. Was not therefore to be seen going out or coming in. When she appeared only in the pastures. Was not therefore to be seen leaving them. Save as though by enchantment. But little by little she began to appear. In the zone of stones. First darkly. Then more and more plain. Till in detail she could be seen crossing the threshold both ways and closing the door behind her. Then a time when within her walls she did not appear. A long time. But little by little she began to appear. Within her walls. Darkly. Time truth to tell still current. Though she within them no more. This long time.

Yes within her walls so far at the window only. At one or the other window. Rapt before the sky. And only half seen so far a pallet and a ghostly chair. Ill half seen. And how in her faint comings and goings she suddenly stops dead. And how hard set to rise up from off her knees. But there too little by little she begins to appear more plain. Within her walls. As well as other objects. Such as under her pillow – such as deep in some recess this still shadowy album. Perhaps in time be by her when she takes it on her knees. See the old fingers fumble through the pages. And what scenes they can possibly be that draw the head down lower still and hold it in thrall. In the meantime who knows no more than withered flowers. No more!

But quick seize her where she is best to be seized. In the pastures far from shelter. She crosses the zone of stones and is there. Clearer and clearer as she goes. Quick seeing she goes out less and less. And so to say only in winter. Winter in her winter haunts she wanders. Far from shelter. Head bowed she makes her slow wavering way across the snow. It is evening. Yet again. On the snow her long shadow keeps her company. The others are there. All about. The twelve. Afar. Still or receding. She raises her eyes and sees one. Turns away and sees another. Again she stops dead. Now the moment or never. But something forbids. Just time to begin to glimpse a fringe of black veil. The face must wait. Just time before the eye cast down. Where nothing to be seen in the grazing rays but snow. And how all about little by little her footprints are effaced.

What is it defends her? Even from her own. Averts

the intent gaze. Incriminates the dearly won. Forbids divining her. What but life ending. Hers. The other's. But so otherwise. She needs nothing. Nothing utterable. Whereas the other. How need in the end? But how? How need in the end?

Times when she is gone. Long lapses of time. At crocus time it would be making for the distant tomb. To have that on the imagination! On top of the rest. Bearing by the stem or round her arm the cross or wreath. But she can be gone at any time. From one moment of the year to the next suddenly no longer there. No longer anywhere to be seen. Nor by the eye of flesh nor by the other. Then as suddenly there again. Long after. So on. Any other would renounce. Avow, No one. No one more. Any other than this other. In wait for her to reappear. In order to resume. Resume the – what is the word? What the wrong word?

Riveted to some detail of the desert the eye fills with tears. Imagination at wit's end spreads its sad wings. Gone she hears one night the sea as if afar. Plucks up her long skirt to make better haste and discovers her boots and stockings to the calf. Tears. Last example the flagstone before her door that by dint by dint her little weight has grooved. Tears.

Before left for the stockings the boots have time to be ill buttoned. Weeping over as weeping will see now the buttonhook larger than life. Of tarnished silver pisciform it hangs by its hook from a nail. It trembles faintly without cease. As if here without cease the earth faintly quaked. The oval handle is wrought to a semblance of scales. The shank a little bent leads up to the hook the eye so far still dry. A lifetime of hooking has lessened its curvature. To the point at certain moments of its seeming unfit for service. Child's play with a pliers to restore it. Was there once a time she did? Careful. Once once in a way. Till she could no more. No more bring the jaws together. Oh not for weakness. Since when it hangs useless from the nail. Trembling imperceptibly without cease. Silver shimmers some evenings when the skies are clear. Close-up then. In which in defiance of reason the nail prevails. Long this image till suddenly it blurs.

She is there. Again. Let the eye from its vigil be distracted a moment. At break or close of day. Distracted by the sky. By something in the sky. So that when it resumes the curtain may be no longer closed. Opened by her to let her see the sky. But even without that she is there. Without the curtain's being opened. Suddenly open. A flash. The suddenness of all! She still without stopping. On her way without starting. Gone without going. Back without returning. Suddenly it is evening. Or dawn. The eye rivets the bare window. Nothing in the sky will distract it from it more. While she from within looks her fill. Pfft occulted. Nothing having stirred.

Already all confusion. Things and imaginings. As of always. Confusion amounting to nothing. Despite precautions. If only she could be pure figment. Unalloyed. This old so dying woman. So dead. In the madhouse of the skull and nowhere else. Where no more precautions to be taken. No precautions possible. Cooped up there with the rest. Hovel and stones. The lot. And the eye. How simple all then. If only all could be pure figment. Neither be nor been nor by any shift to be. Gently gently. On. Careful.

Here to the rescue two lights. Two small skylights. Set in the high-pitched roof on either side. Each shedding dim light. No ceiling therefore. Necessarily. Otherwise with the curtains closed she would be in the dark. Day and night in the dark. And what of it? She is done with raising her eyes. Nearly done. But when she lies with them open she can just make out the rafters. In the dim light the skylights shed. An ever dimmer light. As the panes slowly dimmen. All in black she comes and goes. The hem of her long black skirt brushes the floor. But most often she is still. Standing or sitting. Lying or on her knees. In the dim light the skylights shed. Otherwise with the curtains closed for preference she would be in the dark. In the dark day and night.

Next to emerge from the shadows an inner wall. Only slowly to dissolve in favour of a single space. East the bed. West the chair. A place divided by her use of it alone. How more desirable in every way an interior of a piece. The eye breathes again but not for long. For slowly it emerges again. Rises from the floor and slowly up to lose itself in the gloom. The semigloom. It is evening. The buttonhook glimmers in the last rays. The pallet scarce to be seen.

Weary of the inanimate the eye in her absence falls back on the twelve. Out of her sight as she of theirs. Alone turn where she may she keeps her eyes fixed on the ground. On the way at her feet where it has come to a stop. Winter evening. Not to be precise. All so bygone. To the twelve then for want of better the widowed eye. No matter which. In the distance stiff he stands facing front and the setting sun. Dark greatcoat reaching to the ground. Antiquated block hat. Finally the face caught full in the last rays. Quick enlarge and devour before night falls.

Having no need of light to see the eye makes haste. Before night falls. So it is. So itself belies. Then glutted – then torpid under its lid makes way for unreason. What if not her do they ring around? Careful. She who looks up no more looks up and sees them. Some among them. Still or receding. Receding. Those too closely seen who move to preserve their distance. While at the same time others advance. Those in the wake of her wandering. She never once saw one come toward her. Or she forgets. She forgets. Now some do. Toward but never nearer. Thus they keep her in the centre. More or less. What then if not her do they ring around? In their ring whence she disappears unhindered. Whence they let her disappear. Instead of disappearing in her company. So the unreasoning goes. While the eye digests its pittance. In its private dark. In the general dark.

As hope expires of her ever reappearing she reappears. At first sight little changed. It is evening. It will always be evening. When not night. She emerges at the fringe of the pastures and sets forward across them. Slowly with fluttering step as if wanting mass. Suddenly still and as suddenly on her way again. At this rate it will be black night before she reaches home. Home! But time slows all this while. Suits its speed to hers. Whence from beginning to end of her course no loss or but little of twilight. A matter at most of a candle or two. Bearing south as best she can she casts toward the moon to come her long black shadow. They come at last to the door holding a great key. At the same instant night. When not evening night. Head bowed she stands exposed facing east. All dead still. All save hanging from a finger the old key polished by use. Trembling it faintly shimmers in the light of the moon.

Wooed from below the face consents at last. In the dim light reflected by the flag. Calm slab worn and polished by agelong comings and goings. Livid pallor. Not a wrinkle. How serene it seems this ancient mask. Worthy those worn by certain newly dead. True the light leaves to be desired. The lids occult the longed-for eyes. Time will tell them washen blue. Where tears perhaps not for nothing. Unimaginable tears of old. Lashes jet black remains of the brunette she was. Perhaps once was. When yet a lass. Yet brunette. Skipping the nose at the call of the lips these no sooner broached are withdrawn. The slab having darkened with the darkening sky. Black night henceforward. And at dawn an empty place. With no means of knowing whether she has gone in or under cover of darkness her ways again.

White stones more plentiful every year. As well say every instant. In a fair way if they persist to bury all. First zone rather more extensive than at first sight ill seen and every year rather more. Of striking effect in the light of the moon these millions of little sepulchres. But in her absence but cold comfort. From it then in the end to the second miscalled pastures. Leprous with white scars where the grass has receded from the chalky soil. In contemplation of this erosion the eye finds solace. Everywhere stone is gaining. Whiteness. More and more every year. As well say every instant. Everywhere every instant whiteness is gaining.

The eye will return to the scene of its betrayals. On centennial leave from where tears freeze. Free again an instant to shed them scalding. On the blest tears once shed. While exulting at the white heap of stone. Ever heaping for want of better on itself. Which if it persist will gain the skies. The moon. Venus.

From the stones she steps down into the pastures. As from one tier of a circus to the next. A gap time will fill. For faster than the stones invade it the other ground upheaves its own. So far in silence. A silence time will break. This great silence evening and night. Then all along the verge the muffled thud of stone on stone. Of those spilling their excess on those emergent. Only now and then at first. Then at ever briefer intervals. Till one continuous din. With none to hear. Decreasing as the levels draw together to silence once again. Evening and night. In the meantime she is suddenly sitting with her feet in the pastures. Were it not for the empty hands on the way who knows to the tomb. Back from it then more likely. On the way back from the tomb. Frozen true to her wont she seems turned to stone. Face to the further confines the eye closes in vain to see. At last they appear an instant. North where she passes them always. Shroud of radiant haze. Where to melt into paradise.

The long white hair stares in a fan. Above and about the impassive face. Stares as if shocked still by some ancient horror. Or by its continuance. Or by another. That leaves the face stone-cold. Silence at the eye of the scream. Which say? Ill say. Both. All three. Question answered.

Seated on the stones she is seen from behind. From the waist up. Trunk black rectangle. Nape under frill of black lace. White half halo of hair. Face to the north. The tomb. Eyes on the horizon perhaps. Or closed to see the headstone. The withered crocuses. Endless evening. She lit aslant by the last rays. They make no difference. None to the black of the cloth. None to the white hair. It too dead still. In the still air. Voidlike calm as always. Evening and night. Suffice to watch the grass. How motionless it droops. Till under the relentless eye it shivers. With faintest shiver from its innermost. Equally the hair. Rigidly horrent it shivers at last for the eye about to abandon. And the old body itself. When it seems of stone. Is it not in fact ashiver from head to foot? Let her but go and stand still by the other stone. It white from afar in the pastures. And the eye go from one to the other. Back and forth. What calm then. And what storm. Beneath the weeds' mock calm.

Not possible any longer except as figment. Not endurable. Nothing for it but to close the eye for good and see her. Her and the rest. Close it for good and all and see her to death. Unremittent. In the shack. Over the stones. In the pastures. The haze. At the tomb. And back. And the rest. For good and all. To death. Be shut of it all. On to the next. Next figment. Close it for good this filthy eye of flesh. What forbids? Careful.

Such – such fiasco that folly takes a hand. Such bits and scraps. Seen no matter how and said as seen. Dread of black. Of white. Of void. Let her vanish. And the rest. For good. And the sun. Last rays. And the moon. And Venus. Nothing left but black sky. White earth. Or inversely. No more sky or earth. Finished high and low. Nothing but black and white. Everywhere no matter where. But black. Void. Nothing else. Contemplate that. Not another word. Home at last. Gently gently.

Panic past pass on. The hands. Seen from above. They rest on the pubis intertwined. Strident white. Their faintly leaden tinge killed by the black ground. Suspicion of lace at the wrists. To go with the frill. They tighten then loosen their clasp. Slow systole diastole. And the body that scandal. While its sole hands in view. On its sole pubis. Dead still to be sure. On the chair. After the spectacle. Slowly its spell unbinding. On and on they keep. Tightening and loosening their clasp. Rhythm of a labouring heart. Till when almost despaired of gently part. Suddenly gently. Spreading rise and in midair palms uppermost come to rest. Behold our hollows. Then after a moment as if to hide the lines fall back pronating as they go and light flat on head of thighs. Within an ace of the crotch. It is now the left hand lacks its third finger. A swelling no doubt – a swelling no doubt of the knuckle between first and second phalanges preventing one panic day withdrawal of the ring. The kind called keeper. Still as stones they defy as stones do the eye. Do they as much as feel the clad flesh? Does the clad flesh feel them? Will they then never quiver? This night assuredly not. For before they have – before the eye has time they mist. Who is to blame? Or what? They? The eye? The missing finger? The keeper? The cry? What cry? All five. All six. And the rest. All. All to blame. All.

Winter evening in the pastures. The snow has ceased. Her steps so light they barely leave a trace. Have barely left having ceased. Just enough to be still visible. Adrift the snow. Whither in her head while her feet stray thus? Hither and thither too? Or unswerving to the mirage? And where when she halts? The eye discerns afar a kind of stain. Finally the steep roof whence part of the fresh fall has slid. Under the low lowering sky the north is lost. Obliterated by the snow the twelve are there. Invisible were she to raise her eyes. She on the contrary immaculately black. Not having received a single flake. Nothing needed now but for them to start falling again which therefore they do. First one by one here and there. Then thicker and thicker plumb through the still air. Slowly she disappears. Together with the trace of her steps and that of the distant roof. How find her way home? Home! Even as the homing bird. Safe as the saying is and sound.

All dark in the cabin while she whitens afar. Silence but for the imaginary murmur of flakes beating on the roof. And every now and then a real creak. Her company. Here without having to close the eye sees her afar. Motionless in the snow under the snow. The buttonhook trembles from its nail as if a night like any other. Facing the black curtain the chair exudes its solitude. For want of a fellow-table. Far from it in a corner see suddenly an antique coffer. In its therefore no lesser solitude. It perhaps that creaks. And in its depths who knows the key. The key to close. But this night the chair. Its immovable air. Less than the – more than the empty seat the barred back is piteous. Here if she eats here she sits to eat. The eye closes in the dark and sees her in the end. With her right hand as large as life she holds the edge of the bowl resting on her knees. With her left the spoon dipped in the slop. She waits. For it to cool perhaps. But no. Merely frozen again just as about to begin. At last in a twin movement full of grace she slowly raises the bowl toward her lips while at the same time with equal slowness bowing her head to join it.

Having set out at the same instant they meet halfway and there come to rest. Fresh rigor before the first spoonful slobbered largely back into the slop. Others no happier till time to part lips and bowl and slowly back with never a slip to their starting points. As smooth and even fro as to. Now again the rigid Memnon pose. With her right hand she holds the edge of the bowl. With her left the spoon dipped in the slop. So far so good. But before she can proceed she fades and disappears. Nothing now for the staring eye but the chair in its solitude.

One evening she was followed by a lamb. Reared for slaughter like the others it left them to follow her. In the present to conclude. All so bygone. Slaughter apart it is not like the others. Hanging to the ground in matted coils its fleece hides the little shanks. Rather than walk it seems to glide like a toy in tow. It halts at the same instant as she. At the same instant as she strays on. Stock-still as she it waits with head like hers extravagantly bowed. Clash of black and white that far from muting the last rays amplify. It is now her puniness leaps to the eye. Thanks it would seem to the lowly creature next her. Brief paradox. For suddenly together they move on. Hither and thither toward the stones. There she turns and sits. Does she see the white body at her feet? Head haught now she gazes into emptiness. That profusion. Or with closed eyes sees the tomb. The lamb goes no further. Alone night fallen she makes for home. Home! As straight as were it to be seen.

Was it ever over and done with questions? Dead the whole brood no sooner hatched. Long before. In the egg. Long before. Over and done with answering. With not being able. With not being able not to want to know. With not being able. No. Never. A dream. Question answered.

What remains for the eye exposed to such conditions? To such vicissitude of hardly there and wholly gone. Why none but to open no more. Till all done. She done. Or left undone. Tenement and unreason. No more unless to rest. In the outward and so-called visible. That daub. Quick again to the brim the old nausea and shut again. On her. Till she be whole. Or abort. Question answered.

The coffer. Empty after long nocturnal search. Nothing. Save in the end in a cranny of dust a scrap of paper. Jagged along one edge as if torn from a diary. On its yellowed face in barely legible ink two letters followed by a number. Tu 17. Or Th. Tu or Th 17. Otherwise blank. Otherwise empty.

She reemerges on her back. Dead still. Evening and night. Dead still on her back evening and night. The bed. Careful. A pallet? Hardly if head as ill seen when on her knees. Praying if she prays. Pah she has only to grovel deeper. Or grovel elsewhere. Before the chair. Or the coffer. Or at the edge of the pastures with her head on the stones. A pallet then flat on the floor. No pillow. Hidden from chin to foot under a black covering she offers her face alone. Alone! Face defenceless evening and night. Quick the eyes. The moment they open. Suddenly they are there. Nothing having stirred. One is enough. One staring eye. Gaping pupil thinly nimbed with washen blue. No trace of humour. None any more. Unseeing. As if dazed by what seen behind the lids. The other plumbs its dark. Then opens in its turn. Dazed in its turn.

Incontinent the void. The zenith. Evening again. When not night it will be evening. Death again of deathless day. On the one hand embers. On the other ashes. Day without end won and lost. Unseen.

On resumption the head is covered. No matter. No matter now. Such the confusion now between real and – how say its contrary? No matter. That old tandem. Such now the confusion between them once so twain. And such the farrago from eye to mind. For it to make what sad sense of it may. No matter now. Such equal liars both. Real and – how ill say its contrary? The counter-poison.

Still fresh the coffer fiasco what now of all things but a trapdoor. So cunningly contrived that even to the lidded eye it scarcely shows. Careful. Raise it at once and risk another rebuff? No question. Simply savour in advance with in mind the grisly cupboard its conceivable contents. For the first time then wooden floor. Its boards in line with the trap's designed to conceal it. Promising this flagrant concern with camouflage. But beware. Question by the way what wood of all woods? Ebony why not? Ebony boards. Black on black the brushing skirt. Stark the skeleton chair death-paler than life.

While head included she lies hidden time for a turn in the pastures. No shock were she already dead. As of course she is. But in the meantime more convenient not. Still living then she lies hidden. Having for some reason covered her head. Or for no reason. Night. When not evening night. Winter night. No snow. For the sake of variety. To vary the monotony. The limp grass strangely rigid under the weight of the rime. Clawed by the long black skirt how if but heard it must murmur. Moonless star-studded sky reflected in the erosions filmed with ice. The silence merges into music infinitely far and as unbroken as silence. Ceaseless celestial winds in unison. For all all matters now. The stones gleam faintly afar and the cabin walls seen white at last. Said white. The guardians – the twelve are there but not at full muster. Well! Above all not understand. Simply note how those still faithful have moved apart. Such ill seen that night in the pastures. While head included she lies hidden. Under on closer inspection a long greatcoat. A man's by the buttons. The buttonholes. Eyes closed does she see him?

White walls. High time. White as new. No wind. Not a breath. Unbeaten on by all that comes beating down. And mystery the sun has spared them. The sun that once beat down. So east and west sides the required clash. South gable no problem. But the other. That door. Careful. Black too? Black too. And the roof. Slates. More. Small slates black too brought from a ruined mansion. What tales had they tongues to tell. Their long tale told. Such the dwelling ill seen ill said. Outwardly. High time.

Changed the stone that draws her when revisited alone. Or she who changes it when side by side. Now alone it leans. Backward or forward as the case may be. Is it to nature alone it owes its rough-hewn air? Or to some too human hand forced to desist? As Michelangelo's from the regicide's bust. If there may not be no more questions let there at least be no more answers. Granite of no common variety assuredly. Black as jade the jasper that flecks its whiteness. On its what is the wrong word its uptilted face obscure graffiti. Scrawled by the ages for the eye to solicit in vain. Winter evenings on her doorstep she imagines she can see it glitter afar. When from their source in the west-south-west the last rays rake its averse face. Such ill seen the stone alone where it stands at the far fringe of the pastures. On her way out with the flowers as unerring as best she can she lingers by it. As on her way back with empty hands. Lingers by it a while on her way on. Toward the one or other abode. As unerring as best she can.

See them again side by side. Not quite touching. Lit aslant by the latest last rays they cast to the east-north-east their long parallel shadows. Evening therefore. Winter evening. It will always be evening. Always winter. When not night. Winter night. No more lambs. No more flowers. Empty-handed she shall go to the tomb. Until she go no more. Or no more return. So much for that. Undistinguishable the twin shadows. Till one at length more dense as if of a body better opaque. At length more still. As faintly at length the other trembles under the staring gaze. Throughout this confrontation the sun stands still. That is to say the earth. Not to recoil on until the parting. Then on its face over the pastures and then the stones the still living shadow slowly glides. Lengthening and fading more and more. But never quite away. Under the hovering eye.

Close-up of a dial. Nothing else. White disc divided in minutes. Unless it be in seconds. Sixty black dots. No figure. One hand only. Finest of fine black darts. It advances by fits and starts. No tick. Leaps from dot to dot with so lightning a leap that but for its new position it had not stirred. Whole nights may pass as may but a fraction of a second or any intermediate lapse of time soever before it flings itself from one degree to the next. None at any moment overleaping in all fairness be it said. Let it when discovered be pointing east. Having thus covered after its fashion assuming the instrument plumb the first quarter of its latest hour. Unless it be its latest minute. Then doubt certain – then despair certain nights of its ever attaining the last. Ever regaining north.

She reappears at evening at her window. When not

night evening. If she will see Venus again she must open it. Well! First draw aside the curtain and then open. Head bowed she waits to be able. Mindful perhaps of evenings when she was able too late. Black night fallen. But no. In her head too pure wait. The curtain. Seen closer thanks to this hiatus it reveals itself at last for what it is. A black greatcoat. Hooked by its tails from the rod it hangs sprawling inside out like a carcass in a butcher's stall. Or better inside in for the pathos of the dangling arms. Same infinitesimal quaver as the buttonhook and passim. Another novelty the chair drawn up to the window. This to raise the line of sight on the fair prey loftier when first sighted than at first sight ill seen. What empty space henceforward. For long pacing to and fro in the gloom. Suddenly in a single gesture she snatches aside the coat and to again on a sky as black as it. And then? Careful. Have her sit? Lie? Kneel? Go? She too vacillates. Till in the end the back and forth prevails. Sends her wavering north and south from wall to wall. In the kindly dark.

She is vanishing. With the rest. The already ill seen bedimmed and ill seen again annulled. The mind betrays the treacherous eyes and the treacherous word their treacheries. Haze sole certitude. The same that reigns beyond the pastures. It gains them already. It will gain the zone of stones. Then the dwelling through all its chinks. The eye will close in vain. To see but haze. Not even. Be itself but haze. How can it ever be said? Quick how ever ill said before it submerges all. Light. In one treacherous word. Dazzling haze. Light in its might at last. Where no more to be seen. To be said. Gently gently.

The face yet again in the light of the last rays. No loss of pallor. None of cold. Suspended on the verge for this sight the westering sun. That is the eastering earth. The thin lips seem as if never again to part. Peeping from their join a suspicion of pulp. Unlikely site of olden kisses given and received. Or given only. Or received only. Impressive above all the corners imperceptibly upcurved. A smile? Is it possible? Ghost of an ancient smile smiled finally once and for all. Such ill half seen the mouth in the light of the last rays. Suddenly they leave it. Rather it leaves them. Off again to the dark. There to smile on. If smile is what it is.

Reexamined rid of light the mouth changes. Unexplainably. Lips as before. Same closure. Same hint of extruding pulp. At the corners same imperceptible laxness. In a word the smile still there if smile is what it is. Neither more nor less. Less! And yet no longer the same. True that light distorts. Particularly sunset. That mockery. True too that the eyes then agaze for the viewless planet are now closed. On other viewlessness. Of which more if ever anon. There the explanation at last. This same smile established with eyes open is with them closed no longer the same. Though between the two inspections the mouth unchanged. Utterly. Good. But in what way no longer the same? What there now that was not there? What there no more that was? Enough. Away.

Back after many winters. Long after in this endless winter. This endless heart of winter. Too soon. She as when fled. Where as when fled. Still or again. Eyes closed in the dark. To the dark. In their own dark. On the lips same minute smile. If smile is what it is. In short alive as she alone knows how neither more nor less. Less! Compared to true stone. Within as sadly as before all as at first sight ill seen. With the happy exception of the lights' enhanced opacity. Dim the light of day from them were day again to dawn. Without on the other hand some progress. Toward unbroken night. Universal stone. Day no sooner risen fallen. Scrapped all the ill seen ill said. The eye has changed. And its drivelling scribe. Absence has changed them. Not enough. Time to go again. Where still more to change. Whence back too soon. Changed but not enough. Strangers but not enough. To all the ill seen ill said. Then back again. Disarmed for to finish with it all at last. With her and her rags of sky and earth. And if again too soon go again. Change still more again. Then back again. Barring impediment. Ah. So on. Till fit to finish with it all at last. All the trash. In unbroken night. Universal stone. So first go. But first see her again. As when fled. And the abode. That under the changed eye it too may change. Begin. Just one parting look. Before all meet again. Then go. Barring impediment. Ah.

But see she suddenly no longer there. Where suddenly fled. Quick then the chair before she reappears. At length. Every angle. With what one word convey its change? Careful. Less. Ah the sweet one word. Less. It is less. The same but less. Whencesoever the glare. True that the light. See now how words too. A few drops mishaphazard. Then strangury. To say the least. Less. It will end by being no more. By never having been. Divine prospect. True that the light.

Suddenly enough and way for remembrance. Closed again to that end the vile jelly or opened again or left as it was however that was. Till all recalled. First finally by far hanging from their skirts two black greatcoats. Followed by the first hazy outlines of what possibly a hutch when suddenly enough. Remembrance! When all worse there than when first ill seen. The pallet. The chair. The coffer. The trap. Alone the eye has changed. Alone can cause to change. In the meantime nothing wanting. Wrong. The buttonhook. The nail. Wrong. There they are again. Still. Worse there than ever. Unchanged for the worse. Ope eye and at them to begin. But first the partition. It rid they too would be. It less they by as much.

It of all the properties doubtless the least obdurate. See the instant see it again when unaided it dissolved. So to say of itself. With no help from the eye. Not till long after to reappear. As if reluctantly. For what reason? For one not far to seek. For others then said obscure. One other above all. One other still far to seek. Analogy of the heart? The skull? Hear from here the howls of laughter of the damned.

Enough. Quicker. Quick see how all in keeping with the chair. Minimally less. No more. Well on the way to inexistence. As to zero the infinite. Quick say. And of her? As much. Quick find her again. In that black heart. That mock brain.

The sheet. Between tips of trembling fingers. In two. Four. Eight. Old frantic fingers. Not paper any more. Each eighth apart. In two. Four. Finish with the knife. Hack into shreds. Down the plughole. On to the next. White. Quick blacken.

Alone the face remains. Of the rest beneath its covering no trace. During the inspection a sudden sound. Startling without consequence for the gaze the mind awake. How explain it? And without going so far how say it? Far behind the eye the quest begins. What time the event recedes. When suddenly to the rescue it comes again. Forthwith the uncommon common noun collapsion. Reinforced a little later if not enfeebled by the infrequent slumberous. A slumberous collapsion. Two. Then far from the still agonizing eye a gleam of hope. By the grace of these modest beginnings. With in second sight the shack in ruins. To scrute together with the inscrutable face. All curiosity spent.

Later while the face still unyielding another sound of fall but this time sharp. Heightening the fond illusion of general havoc in train. Here a great leap into what brief future remains and summary puncture of that puny balloon. Far ahead to the instant when the coats will have gone from their rods and the buttonhook from its nail. And been hove the sigh no more than that. Sigh upon sigh till all sighed quite away. All the fond trash. Destined before being to be no more than that. Last sighs. Of relief.

Quick beforehand again two mysteries. Not even. Mild shocks. Not even. In such abeyance the mind then. And from then on. First the curtains gone without loss of dark. Sweet foretaste of the joy at journey's end. Second after long hesitation no trace of the fallen where they fell. No trace of all the ado. Alone on the one hand the rods alone. A little bent. And alone on the other most alone the nail. Unimpaired. All set to serve again. Like unto its glorious ancestors. At the place of the skull. One April afternoon. Deposition done.

Full glare now on the face present throughout the recent future. As seen ill seen throughout the past neither more nor less. Less! Collated with its cast it lives beyond a doubt. Were it only by virtue of its imperfect pallor. And imperceptible tremor unworthy of true plaster. Heartening on the other hand the eyes persistently closed. No doubt a record in this position. Unobserved at least till now. Suddenly the look. Nothing having stirred. Look?

Too weak a word. Too wrong. Its absence? No better.
Unspeakable globe. Unbearable.

Ample time none the less a few seconds for the iris
to be lacking. Wholly. As if engulfed by the pupil. And
for the sclerotic not to say the white to appear
reduced by half. Already that much less at least but
at what cost. Soon to be foreseen save unforeseen two
black blanks. Fit ventholes of the soul that jakes.
Here reappearance of the skylights opaque to no purpose henceforward. Seeing the black night or better
blackness pure and simple that limpid they would
shed. Blackness in its might at last. Where no more to
be seen. Perforce to be seen.

Absence supreme good and yet. Illumination then
go again and on return no more trace. On earth's face.
Of what was never. And if by mishap some left then go
again. For good again. So on. Till no more trace. On
earth's face. Instead of always the same place. Slaving
away forever in the same place. At this and that trace.
And what if the eye could not? No more tear itself
away from the remains of trace. Of what was never.
Quick say it suddenly can and farewell say say
farewell. If only to the face. Of her tenacious trace.

Decision no sooner reached or rather long after

than what is the wrong word? For the last time at last for to end yet again what the wrong word? Than revoked. No but slowly dispelled a little very little like the last wisps of day when the curtain closes. Of itself by slow millimetres or drawn by a phantom hand. Farewell to farewell. Then in that perfect dark foreknell darling sound pip for end begun. First last moment. Grant only enough remain to devour all. Moment by glutton moment. Sky earth the whole kit and boodle. Not another crumb of carrion left. Lick chops and basta. No. One moment more. One last. Grace to breathe that void. Know happiness.

Worstward Ho

On. Say on. Be said on. Somehow on. Till nohow on. Said nohow on.

Say for be said. Missaid. From now say for be missaid.

Say a body. Where none. No mind. Where none. That at least. A place. Where none. For the body. To be in. Move in. Out of. Back into. No. No out. No back. Only in. Stay in. On in. Still.

All of old. Nothing else ever. Ever tried. Ever failed. No matter. Try again. Fail again. Fail better.

First the body. No. First the place. No. First both. Now either. Now the other. Sick of the either try the other. Sick of it back sick of the either. So on. Somehow on. Till sick of both. Throw up and go. Where neither. Till sick of there. Throw up and back. The body again. Where none. The place again. Where none. Try again. Fail again. Better again. Or better worse. Fail worse again. Still worse again. Till sick for good. Throw up for good. Go for good. Where neither for good. Good and all.

It stands. What? Yes. Say it stands. Had to up in the end and stood. Say bones. No bones but say bones. Say ground. No ground but say ground. So as to say pain. No mind and pain? Say yes that the bones may pain till no choice but stand. Somehow up and stand. Or better worse remains. Say remains of mind where none to permit of pain. Pain of bones till no choice but up and stand. Somehow up. Somehow stand. Remains of mind where none for the sake of pain. Here of bones. Other examples if needs must. Of pain. Relief from. Change of.

All of old. Nothing else ever. But never so failed. Worse failed. With care never worse failed.

Dim light source unknown. Know minimum. Know nothing no. Too much to hope. At most mere minimum. Meremost minimum.

No choice but stand. Somehow up and stand. Somehow stand. That or groan. The groan so long on its way. No. No groan. Simply pain. Simply up. A time when try how. Try see. Try say. How first it lay. Then somehow knelt. Bit by bit. Then on from there. Bit by bit. Till up at last. Not now. Fail better worse now.

Another. Say another. Head sunk on crippled hands. Vertex vertical. Eyes clenched. Seat of all. Germ of all.

No future in this. Alas yes.

It stands. See in the dim void how at last it stands. In the dim light source unknown. Before the downcast eyes. Clenched eyes. Staring eyes. Clenched staring eyes.

That shade. Once lying. Now standing. That a body? Yes. Say that a body. Somehow standing. In the dim void.

A place. Where none. A time when try see. Try say. How small. How vast. How if not boundless bounded. Whence the dim. Not now. Know better now. Unknow better now. Know only no out of. No knowing how know only no out of. Into only. Hence another. Another place where none. Whither once whence no return. No. No place but the one. None but the one where none. Whence never once in. Somehow in. Beyondless. Thenceless there. Thitherless there. Thenceless thitherless there.

Where then but there see –

See for be seen. Misseen. From now see for be misseen.

Where then but there see now –

First back turned the shade astand. In the dim void see first back turned the shade astand. Still.

Where then but there see now another. Bit by bit an old man and child. In the dim void bit by bit an old man and child. Any other would do as ill.

Hand in hand with equal plod they go. In the free hands – no. Free empty hands. Backs turned both bowed with equal plod they go. The child hand raised to reach the holding hand. Hold the old holding hand. Hold and be held. Plod on and never recede. Slowly with never a pause plod on and never recede. Backs turned. Both bowed. Joined by held holding hands. Plod on as one. One shade. Another shade.

Head sunk on crippled hands. Clenched staring eyes. At in the dim void shades. One astand at rest. One old man and child. At rest plodding on. Any others would do as ill. Almost any. Almost as ill.

They fade. Now the one. Now the twain. Now

both. Fade back. Now the one. Now the twain. Now both. Fade? No. Sudden go. Sudden back. Now the one. Now the twain. Now both.

Unchanged? Sudden back unchanged? Yes. Say yes. Each time unchanged. Somehow unchanged. Till no. Till say no. Sudden back changed. Somehow changed. Each time somehow changed.

The dim. The void. Gone too? Back too? No. Say no. Never gone. Never back. Till yes. Till say yes. Gone too. Back too. The dim. The void. Now the one. Now the other. Now both. Sudden gone. Sudden back. Unchanged? Sudden back unchanged? Yes. Say yes. Each time unchanged. Somehow unchanged. Till no. Till say no. Sudden back changed. Somehow changed. Each time somehow changed.

First sudden gone the one. First sudden back. Unchanged. Say now unchanged. So far unchanged. Back turned. Head sunk. Vertex vertical in hat. Cocked back of black brim alone. Back of black greatcoat cut off midthigh. Kneeling. Better kneeling. Better worse kneeling. Say now kneeling. From now kneeling. Could rise but to its knees. Sudden gone sudden back unchanged back turned head sunk dark shade on unseen knees. Still.

Next sudden gone the twain. Next sudden back. Unchanged. Say now unchanged. So far unchanged. Backs turned. Heads sunk. Dim hair. Dim white and hair so fair that in that dim light dim white. Black greatcoats to heels. Dim black. Bootheels. Now the two right. Now the two left. As on with equal plod they go. No ground. Plod as on void. Dim hands. Dim white. Two free and two as one. So sudden gone sudden back unchanged as one dark shade plod unreceding on.

The dim. Far and wide the same. High and low. Unchanging. Say now unchanging. Whence no knowing. No saying. Say only such dim light as never. On all. Say a grot in that void. A gulf. Then in that grot or gulf such dimmest light as never. Whence no knowing. No saying.

The void. Unchanging. Say now unchanging. Void were not the one. The twain. So far were not the one and twain. So far.

The void. How try say? How try fail? No try no fail. Say only –

First the bones. On back to them. Preying since first said on foresaid remains. The ground. The pain.

No bones. No ground. No pain. Why up unknown. At all costs unknown. If ever down. No choice but up if ever down. Or never down. Forever kneeling. Better forever kneeling. Better worse forever kneeling. Say from now forever kneeling. So far from now forever kneeling. So far.

The void. Before the staring eyes. Stare where they may. Far and wide. High and low. That narrow field. Know no more. See no more. Say no more. That alone. That little much of void alone.

On back to unsay void can go. Void cannot go. Save dim go. Then all go. All not already gone. Till dim back. Then all back. All not still gone. The one can go. The twain can go. Dim can go. Void cannot go. Save dim go. Then all go.

On back better worse to fail the head said seat of all. Germ of all. All? If of all of it too. Where if not there it too? There in the sunken head the sunken head. The hands. The eyes. Shade with the other shades. In the same dim. The same narrow void. Before the staring eyes. Where it too if not there too? Ask not. No. Ask in vain. Better worse so.

The head. Ask not if it can go. Say no. Unasking

no. It cannot go. Save dim go. Then all go. Oh dim go.
Go for good. All for good. Good and all.

Whose words? Ask in vain. Or not in vain if say
no knowing. No saying. No words for him whose
words. Him? One. No words for one whose words.
One? It. No words for it whose words. Better worse
so.

Something not wrong with one. Meaning – meaning! – meaning the kneeling one. From now one for
the kneeling one. As from now two for the twain. The
as one plodding twain. As from now three for the
head. The head as first said missaid. So from now.
For to gain time. Time to lose. Gain time to lose. As
the soul once. The world once.

Something not wrong with one. Then with two.
Then with three. So on. Something not wrong with
all. Far from wrong. Far far from wrong.

The words too whosesoever. What room for
worse! How almost true they sometimes almost ring!
How wanting in inanity! Say the night is young alas
and take heart. Or better worse say still a watch of
night alas to come. A rest of last watch to come. And
take heart.

First one. First try fail better one. Something there badly not wrong. Not that as it is it is not bad. The no face bad. The no hands bad. The no –. Enough. A pox on bad. Mere bad. Way for worse. Pending worse still. First worse. Mere worse. Pending worse still. Add a –. Add? Never. Bow it down. Be it bowed down. Deep down. Head in hat gone. More back gone. Greatcoat cut off higher. Nothing from pelvis down. Nothing but bowed back. Topless baseless hindtrunk. Dim black. On unseen knees. In the dim void. Better worse so. Pending worse still.

Next try fail better two. The twain. Bad as it is as it is. Bad the no –

First back on to three. Not yet to try worsen. Simply be there again. There in that head in that head. Be it again. That head in that head. Clenched eyes clamped to it alone. Alone? No. Too. To it too. The sunken skull. The crippled hands. Clenched staring eyes. Clenched eyes clamped to clenched staring eyes. Be that shade again. In that shade again. With the other shades. Worsening shades. In the dim void.

Next –

First how all at once. In that stare. The worsened

one. The worsening two. And what yet to worsen. To try worsen. Itself. The dim. The void. All at once in that stare. Clenched eyes clamped to all.

Next two. From bad to worsen. Try worsen. From merely bad. Add –. Add? Never. The boots. Better worse bootless. Bare heels. Now the two right. Now the two left. Left right left right on. Barefoot unreceding on. Better worse so. A little better worse than nothing so.

Next the so-said seat and germ of all. Those hands! That head! That near true ring! Away. Full face from now. No hands. No face. Skull and stare alone. Scene and seer of all.

On. Stare on. Say on. Be on. Somehow on. Anyhow on. Till dim gone. At long last gone. All at long last gone. For bad and all. For poor best worse and all.

Dim whence unknown. At all costs unknown. Unchanging. Say now unchanging. Far and wide. High and low. Say a pipe in that void. A tube. Sealed. Then in that pipe or tube that selfsame dim. Old dim. When ever what else? Where all always to be seen. Of the nothing to be seen. Dimly seen. Nothing

ever unseen. Of the nothing to be seen. Dimly seen.
Worsen that?

Next the so-said void. The so-missaid. That narrow field. Rife with shades. Well so-missaid. Shade-
ridden void. How better worse so-missay?

Add others. Add? Never. Till if needs must.
Nothing to those so far. Dimly so far. Them only
lessen. But with them as they lessen others. As they
worsen. If needs must. Others to lessen. To worsen.
Till dim go. At long last go. For worst and all.

On. Somehow on. Anyhow on. Say all gone. So
on. In the skull all gone. All? No. All cannot go. Till
dim go. Say then but the two gone. In the skull one
and two gone. From the void. From the stare. In the
skull all save the skull gone. The stare. Alone in the
dim void. Alone to be seen. Dimly seen. In the skull
the skull alone to be seen. The staring eyes. Dimly
seen. By the staring eyes. The others gone. Long sudden gone. Then sudden back. Unchanged. Say now
unchanged. First one. Then two. Or first two. Then
one. Or together. Then all again together. The bowed
back. The plodding twain. The skull. The stare. All
back in the skull together. Unchanged. Stare
clamped to all. In the dim void.

The eyes. Time to –

First on back to unsay dim can go. Somehow on
back. Dim cannot go. Dim to go must go for good.
True then dim can go. If but for good. One can go
not for good. Two too. Three no if not for good. With
dim gone for good. Void no if not for good. With all
gone for good. Dim can worsen. Somehow worsen.
Go no. If not for good.

The eyes. Time to try worsen. Somehow try wors-
en. Unclench. Say staring open. All white and pupil.
Dim white. White? No. All pupil. Dim black holes.
Unwavering gaping. Be they so said. With worsening
words. From now so. Better than nothing so bettered
for the worse.

Still dim still on. So long as still dim still somehow
on. Anyhow on. With worsening words. Worsening
stare. For the nothing to be seen. At the nothing to
be seen. Dimly seen. As now by way of somehow on
where in the nowhere all together? All three together.
Where there all three as last worse seen? Bowed back
alone. Barefoot plodding twain. Skull and lidless
stare. Where in the narrow vast? Say only vasts apart.
In that narrow void vasts of void apart. Worse better
later.

What when words gone? None for what then. But say by way of somehow on somehow with sight to do. With less of sight. Still dim and yet –. No. Nohow so on. Say better worse words gone when nohow on. Still dim and nohow on. All seen and nohow on. What words for what then? None for what then. No words for what when words gone. For what when nohow on. Somehow nohow on.

Worsening words whose unknown. Whence unknown. At all costs unknown. Now for to say as worst they may only they only they. Dim void shades all they. Nothing save what they say. Somehow say. Nothing save they. What they say. Whosesoever whencesoever say. As worst they may fail ever worse to say.

Remains of mind then still. Enough still. Somewhose somewhere somehow enough still. No mind and words? Even such words. So enough still. Just enough still to joy. Joy! Just enough still to joy that only they. Only!

Enough still not to know. Not to know what they say. Not to know what it is the words it says say. Says? Secretes. Say better worse secretes. What it is the words it secretes say. What the so-said void.

The so-said dim. The so-said shades. The so-said seat and germ of all. Enough to know no knowing. No knowing what it is the words it secretes say. No saying. No saying what it all is they somehow say.

That said on back to try worse say the plodding twain. Preying since last worse said on foresaid remains. But what not on them preying? What seen? What said? What of all seen and said not on them preying? True. True! And yet say worst perhaps worst of all the old man and child. That shade as last worse seen. Left right left right barefoot unreceding on. They then the words. Back to them now for want of better on and better fail. Worser fail that perhaps of all the least. Least worse failed of all the worse failed shades. Less worse than the bowed back alone. The skull and lidless stare. Though they too for worse. But what not for worse. True. True! And yet say first the worst perhaps worst of all the old man and child. Worst in need of worse. Worse in –

Blanks for nohow on. How long? Blanks how long till somehow on? Again somehow on. All gone when nohow on. Time gone when nohow on.

Worse less. By no stretch more. Worse for want of

better less. Less best. No. Naught best. Best worse. No. Not best worse. Naught not best worse. Less best worse. No. Least. Least best worse. Least never to be naught. Never to naught be brought. Never by naught be nulled. Unnullable least. Say that best worse. With leastening words say least best worse. For want of worser worst. Unlessenable least best worse.

The twain. The hands. Held holding hands. That almost ring! As when first said on crippled hands the head. Crippled hands! They there then the words. Here now held holding. As when first said. Ununsaid when worse said. Away. Held holding hands!

The empty too. Away. No hands in the –. No. Save for worse to say. Somehow worse somehow to say. Say for now still seen. Dimly seen. Dim white. Two dim white empty hands. In the dim void.

So leastward on. So long as dim still. Dim undimmed. Or dimmed to dimmer still. To dimmost dim. Leastmost in dimmost dim. Utmost dim. Leastmost in utmost dim. Unworsenable worst.

What words for what then? How almost they still ring. As somehow from some soft of mind they ooze.

From it in it ooze. How all but uninane. To last unlessenable least how loath to leasten. For then in utmost dim to unutter leastmost all.

So little worse the old man and child. Gone held holding hands they plod apart. Left right barefoot unreceding on. Not worsen yet the rift. Save for some after nohow somehow worser on.

On back to unsay clamped to all the stare. No but from now to now this and now that. As now from worsened twain to next for worse alone. To skull and stare alone. Of the two worse in want the skull preying since unsunk. Now say the fore alone. No dome. Temple to temple alone. Clamped to it and stare alone the stare. Bowed back alone and twain blurs in the void. So better than nothing worse shade three from now.

Somehow again on back to the bowed back alone. Nothing to show a woman's and yet a woman's. Oozed from softening soft the word woman's. The words old woman's. The words nothing to show bowed back alone a woman's and yet a woman's. So better worse from now that shade a woman's. An old woman's.

Next fail see say how dim undimmed to worsen.

How nohow save to dimmer still. But but a shade so as when after nohow somehow on to dimmer still. Till dimmost dim. Best bad worse of all. Save somehow undimmed worser still.

Ooze on back not to unsay but say again the vasts apart. Say seen again. No worse again. The vasts of void apart. Of all so far missaid the worse missaid. So far. Not till nohow worse missay say worse missaid. Not till for good nohow on poor worst missaid.

Longing the so-said mind long lost to longing. The so-missaid. So far so-missaid. Dint of long longing lost to longing. Long vain longing. And longing still. Faintly longing still. Faintly vainly longing still. For fainter still. For faintest. Faintly vainly longing for the least of longing. Unlessenable least of longing. Unstillable vain last of longing still.

Longing that all go. Dim go. Void go. Longing go. Vain longing that vain longing go.

Said is missaid. Whenever said said said missaid. From now said alone. No more from now now said and now missaid. From now said alone. Said for missaid. For be missaid.

Back is on. Somehow on. From now back alone. No more from now now back and now back on. From now back alone. Back for back on. Back for somehow on.

Back unsay better worse by no stretch more. If more dim less light then better worse more dim. Unsaid then better worse by no stretch more. Better worse may no less than less be more. Better worse what? The say? The said. Same thing. Same nothing. Same all but nothing.

No once. No once in pastless now. No not none. When before worse the shades? The dim before more? When if not once. Onceless alone the void. By no stretch more. By none less. Onceless till no more.

Ooze back try worsen blanks. Those then when nohow on. Unsay then all gone. All not gone. Only nohow on. All not gone and nohow on. All there as now when somehow on. The dim. The void. The shades. Only words gone. Ooze gone. Till ooze again and on. Somehow ooze on.

Preying since last worse the stare. Something there still far so far from wrong. So far far far from wrong. Try better worse another stare when with words than when not. When somehow than when nohow. While all seen the same. No not all seen the same. Seen other. By the same other stare seen other. When with words than when not. When somehow than when nohow. How fail say how other seen?

Less. Less seen. Less seeing. Less seen and seeing when with words than when not. When somehow than when nohow. Stare by words dimmed. Shades dimmed. Void dimmed. Dim dimmed. All there as when no words. As when nohow. Only all dimmed. Till blank again. No words again. Nohow again. Then all undimmed. Stare undimmed. That words had dimmed.

Back unsay shades can go. Go and come again. No. Shades cannot go. Much less come again. Nor bowed old woman's back. Nor old man and child. Nor foreskull and stare. Blur yes. Shades can blur. When stare clamped to one alone. Or somehow words again. Go no nor come again. Till dim if ever go. Never to come again.

Blanks for when words gone. When nohow on. Then all seen as only then. Undimmed. All undimmed that words dim. All so seen unsaid. No ooze then. No trace on soft when from it ooze again.

In it ooze again. Ooze alone for seen as seen with ooze. Dimmed. No ooze for seen undimmed. For when nohow on. No ooze for when ooze gone.

Back try worsen twain preying since last worse. Since atwain. Two once so one. From now rift a vast. Vast of void atween. With equal plod still unreceding on. That little better worse. Till words for worser still. Worse words for worser still.

Preying but what not preying? When not preying? Nohow over words again say what then when not preying. Each better worse for naught. No stilling preying. The shades. The dim. The void. All always faintly preying. Worse for naught. Worser for naught. No less than when but bad all always faintly preying. Gnawing.

Gnawing to be gone. Less no good. Worse no good. Only one good. Gone. Gone for good. Till then gnaw on. All gnaw on. To be gone.

All save void. No. Void too. Unworsenable void. Never less. Never more. Never since first said never unsaid never worse said never not gnawing to be gone.

Say child gone. As good as gone. From the void.

From the stare. Void then not that much more? Say old man gone. Old woman gone. As good as gone. Void then not that much more again? No. Void most when almost. Worst when almost. Less then? All shades as good as gone. If then not that much more then that much less then? Less worse then? Enough. A pox on void. Unmoreable unlessable unworseable evermost almost void.

Back to once so-said two as one. Preying ever since not long since last failed worse. Ever since vast atween. Say better worse now all gone save trunks from now. Nothing from pelves down. From napes up. Topless baseless hindtrunks. Legless plodding on. Left right unreceding on.

Stare clamped to stare. Bowed backs blurs in stare clamped to stare. Two black holes. Dim black. In through skull to soft. Out from soft through skull. Agape in unseen face. That the flaw? The want of flaw? Try better worse set in skull. Two black holes in foreskull. Or one. Try better still worse one. One dim black hole mid-foreskull. Into the hell of all. Out from the hell of all. So better than nothing worse say stare from now.

Stare outstared away to old man hindtrunk

unreceding on. Try better worse kneeling. Legs gone say better worse kneeling. No more if ever on. Say never. Say never on. Ever kneeling. Legs gone from stare say better worse ever kneeling. Stare away to child and worsen same. Vast void apart old man and child dim shades on unseen knees. One blur. One clear. Dim clear. Now the one. Now the other.

Nothing to show a child and yet a child. A man and yet a man. Old and yet old. Nothing but ooze how nothing and yet. One bowed back yet an old man's. The other yet a child's. A small child's.

Somehow again and all in stare again. All at once as once. Better worse all. The three bowed down. The stare. The whole narrow void. No blurs. All clear. Dim clear. Black hole agape on all. Inletting all. Outletting all.

Nothing and yet a woman. Old and yet old. On unseen knees. Stooped as loving memory some old gravestones stoop. In that old graveyard. Names gone and when to when. Stoop mute over the graves of none.

Same stoop for all. Same vasts apart. Such last

state. Latest state. Till somehow less in vain. Worse in vain. All gnawing to be naught. Never to be naught.

What were skull to go? As good as go. Into what then black hole? From out what then? What why of all? Better worse so? No. Skull better worse. What left of skull. Of soft. Worst why of all of all. So skull not go. What left of skull not go. Into it still the hole. Into what left of soft. From out what little left.

Enough. Sudden enough. Sudden all far. No move and sudden all far. All least. Three pins. One pinhole. In dimmost dim. Vasts apart. At bounds of boundless void. Whence no farther. Best worse no farther. Nohow less. Nohow worse. Nohow naught. Nohow on.

Said nohow on.

Stirrings Still

for Barney Rosset

I

One night as he sat at his table head on hands he
saw himself rise and go. One night or day. For when
his own light went out he was not left in the dark.
Light of a kind came then from the one high window.
Under it still the stool on which till he could or would
no more he used to mount to see the sky. Why he did
not crane out to see what lay beneath was perhaps
because the window was not made to open or
because he could or would not open it. Perhaps he
knew only too well what lay beneath and did not wish
to see it again. So he would simply stand there high
above the earth and see through the clouded pane
the cloudless sky. Its faint unchanging light unlike
any light he could remember from the days and
nights when day followed hard on night and night on
day. This outer light then when his own went out
became his only light till it in its turn went out and
left him in the dark. Till it in its turn went out.

One night or day then as he sat at his table head
on hands he saw himself rise and go. First rise and
stand clinging to the table. Then sit again. Then rise
again and stand clinging to the table again. Then go.
Start to go. On unseen feet start to go. So slow that

only change of place to show he went. As when he disappeared only to reappear later at another place. Then disappeared again only to reappear again later at another place again. So again and again disappeared again only to reappear again later at another place again. Another place in the place where he sat at his table head on hands. The same place and table as when Darly for example died and left him. As when others too in their turn before and since. As when others would too in their turn and leave him till he too in his turn. Head on hands half hoping when he disappeared again that he would not reappear again and half fearing that he would not. Or merely wondering. Or merely waiting. Waiting to see if he would or would not. Leave him or not alone again waiting for nothing again.

Seen always from behind whithersoever he went. Same hat and coat as of old when he walked the roads. The back roads. Now as one in a strange place seeking the way out. In the dark. In a strange place blindly in the dark of night or day seeking the way out. A way out. To the roads. The back roads.

A clock afar struck the hours and half-hours. The same as when among others Darly once died and left him. Strokes now clear as if carried by a wind now faint on the still air. Cries afar now faint now clear. Head on hands half hoping when the hour struck that the half-hour would not and half fearing that it would not. Similarly when the half-hour struck. Similarly when the cries a moment ceased. Or merely wondering. Or merely waiting. Waiting to hear.

There had been a time he would sometimes lift his head enough to see his hands. What of them was to be seen. One laid on the table and the other on the one. At rest after all they did. Lift his past head a moment to see his past hands. Then lay it back on them to rest it too. After all it did.

The same place as when left day after day for the roads. The back roads. Returned to night after night. Paced from wall to wall in the dark. The then fleeting dark of night. Now as if strange to him seen to rise and go. Disappear and reappear at another place. Disappear again and reappear again at another place again. Or at the same. Nothing to show not the same. No wall toward which or from. No table back toward which or further from. In the same place as when paced from wall to wall all places as the same. Or in another. Nothing to show not another. Where never. Rise and go in the same place as ever. Disappear and reappear in another where never. Nothing to show not another where never. Nothing but the strokes. The cries. The same as ever.

Till so many strokes and cries since he was last seen that perhaps he would not be seen again. Then so many cries since the strokes were last heard that perhaps they would not be heard again. Then such silence since the cries were last heard that perhaps even they would not be heard again. Perhaps thus the end. Unless no more than a mere lull. Then all as before. The strokes and cries as before and he as before now there now gone now there again now gone again. Then the lull again. Then all as before again. So again and again. And patience till the one true end to time and grief and self and second self his own.

2

As one in his right mind when at last out again he knew not how he was not long out again when he began to wonder if he was in his right mind. For could one not in his right mind be reasonably said to wonder if he was in his right mind and bring what is more his remains of reason to bear on this perplexity in the way he must be said to do if he is to be said at all? It was therefore in the guise of a more or less reasonable being that he emerged at last he knew not how into the outer world and had not been there for more than six or seven hours by the clock when he could not but begin to wonder if he was in his right mind. By the same clock whose strokes were those heard times without number in his confinement as it struck the hours and half-hours and so in a sense at first a source of reassurance till finally one of alarm as being no clearer now than when in principle muffled by his four walls. Then he sought help in the thought of one hastening westward at sundown to obtain a better view of Venus and found it of none. Of the sole other sound that of cries enlivener of his solitude as lost to suffering he sat at his table head on hands the same was true. Of their whenceabouts that is of clock and cries the same was true that is no more

to be determined now than as was only natural then.
Bringing to bear on all this his remains of reason he
sought help in the thought that his memory of
indoors was perhaps at fault and found it of none.
Further to his disarray his soundless tread as when
barefoot he trod his floor. So all ears from bad to
worse till in the end he ceased if not to hear to listen
and set out to look about him. Result finally he was
in a field of grass which went some way if nothing
else to explain his tread and then a little later as if to
make up for this some way to increase his trouble.
For he could recall no field of grass from even the
very heart of which no limit of any kind was to be discovered but always in some quarter or another some
end in sight such as a fence or other manner of
bourne from which to return. Nor on his looking
more closely to make matters worse was this the
short green grass he seemed to remember eaten
down by flocks and herds but long and light grey in
colour verging here and there on white. Then he
sought help in the thought that his memory of out-
doors was perhaps at fault and found it of none. So
all eyes from bad to worse till in the end he ceased if
not to see to look (about him or more closely) and set
out to take thought. To this end for want of a stone
on which to sit like Walther and cross his legs the best
he could do was stop dead and stand stock still which

after a moment of hesitation he did and of course sink his head as one deep in meditation which after another moment of hesitation he did also. But soon weary of vainly delving in those remains he moved on through the long hoar grass resigned to not knowing where he was or how he got there or where he was going or how to get back to whence he knew not how he came. So on unknowing and no end in sight. Unknowing and what is more no wish to know nor indeed any wish of any kind nor therefore any sorrow save that he would have wished the strokes to cease and the cries for good and was sorry that they did not. The strokes now faint now clear as if carried by the wind but not a breath and the cries now faint now clear.

3

So on till stayed when to his ears from deep with-in oh how and here a word he could not catch it were to end where never till then. Rest then before again from not long to so long that perhaps never again and then again faint from deep within oh how and here that missing word again it were to end where never till then. In any case whatever it might be to end and so on was he not already as he stood there all bowed down and to his ears faint from deep within again and again oh how something and so on was he not so far as he could see already there where never till then? For how could even such a one as he having once found himself in such a place not shudder to find himself in it again which he had not done nor having shuddered seek help in vain in the thought so-called that having somehow got out of it then he could somehow get out of it again which he had not done either. There then all this time where never till then and so far as he could see in every direction when he raised his head and opened his eyes no danger or hope as the case might be of his ever getting out of it. Was he then now to press on regardless now in one direction and now in another or on the other hand stir no more as the case might be that is as that

missing word might be which if to warn such as sad
or bad for example then of course in spite of all the
one and if the reverse then of course the other that is
stir no more. Such and much more such the hubbub
in his mind so-called till nothing left from deep within but only ever fainter oh to end. No matter how no
matter where. Time and grief and self so-called. Oh
all to end.

One Evening

He was found lying on the ground. No one had missed him. No one was looking for him. An old woman found him. To put it vaguely. It happened so long ago. She was straying in search of wild flowers. Yellow only. With no eyes but for these she stumbled on him lying there. He lay face downward and arms outspread. He wore a greatcoat in spite of the time of year. Hidden by the body a long row of buttons fastened it all the way down. Buttons of all shapes and sizes. Worn upright the skirts swept the ground. That seems to hang together. Near the head a hat lay askew on the ground. At once on its brim and crown. He lay inconspicuous in the greenish coat. To catch an eye searching from afar there was only the white head. May she have seen him somewhere before? Somewhere on his feet before? Not too fast. She was all in black. The hem of her long black skirt trailed in the grass. It was close of day. Should she now move away into the east her shadow would go before. A long black shadow. It was lambing time. But there were no lambs. She could see none. Were a third party to chance that way theirs were the only bodies he would see. First that of the old woman standing. Then on drawing near it lying on the ground. That seems to hang together. The deserted fields. The old woman all in black stock-still. The body stock-still on the ground. Yellow at the end of the black arm. The white hair in the grass. The east foundering in night. Not too fast. The weather. Sky overcast all day till evening. In the west-north-west near the verge already the sun came out at last. Rain? A few drops if you will. A few drops in the morning if you will. In the present to conclude. It happened so long ago. Cooped indoors all day she comes out with the sun. She makes haste to gain the fields. Surprised to have seen no one on the way she strays feverishly in search of the wild flowers. Feverishly seeing the imminence of night. She remarks with surprise the absence of lambs in great numbers here at this time of year. She is wearing the black she took on when widowed young. It is to reflower the grave she strays in search of the flowers he had loved. But for the need of yellow at the end of the black arm there would be none. There are therefore only as few as possible. This is for her the third surprise since she came out. For they grow in plenty here at this time of year. Her old friend her shadow irks her. So much so that she turns to face the sun. Any flower wide of her course she reaches sidelong. She craves for sundown to end and to stray freely again in the long afterglow. Further to her distress the familiar rustle of her long black skirt in the grass. She moves with half-closed eyes as if drawn on into the glare. She may say to herself it is too much strangeness for a single March or April evening. No one abroad. Not a single lamb. Scarcely a flower. Shadow and rustle irksome. And to crown all the shock of her foot against a body. Chance. No one had missed him. No one was looking for him. Black and green of the garments touching now. Near the white head the yellow of the few plucked flowers. The old sunlit face. Tableau vivant if you will. In its way. All is silent from now on. For as long as she cannot move. The sun disappears at last and with it all shadow. All shadow here. Slow fade of afterglow. Night without moon or stars. All that seems to hang together. But no more about it.

The Way

The way wound up from foot to top and thence
on down another way. On back down. The ways
crossed midway more and less. A little more and less
than midway up and down. The ways were one-way.
No retracing the way up back down nor back up the
way down. Neither in whole from top or foot nor in
part from on the way. The one way back was on and
on was always back. Freedom once at foot and top to
pause or not. Before on back up and down. Briefly
once at the extremes the will set free. Gait down as
up same plod always. A foot a second or mile an hour
and more. So from foot and top to crossways could
the seconds have been numbered then height known
and depth. Could but those seconds have been numbered. Thorns hemmed the way. The ways. Same
mist always. Same half-light. As were the earth at
rest. Loose sand underfoot. So no sign of remains no
sign that none before. No one ever before so –

∞

Forth and back across a barren same winding
one-way way. Low in the west or east the sun standstill. As if the earth at rest. Long shadows before and

after. Same pace and countless time. Same ignorance of how far. Same leisure once at either end to pause or not. At either groundless end. Before back forth or back. Through emptiness the beaten ways as fixed as if enclosed. Were the eye to look unending void. In unending ending or beginning light. Bedrock underfoot. So no sign of remains a sign that none before. No one ever before so –

Ceiling

For Avigdor
September 1981

On coming to the first sight is of white. Some time after coming to the first sight is of dull white. For some time after coming to the eyes continue to. When in the end they open they are met by this dull white. Consciousness eyes to of having come to. When in the end they open they are met by this dull white. Dim consciousness eyes bidden to of having come partly to. When in the end bidden they open they are met by this dull white. Dim consciousness eyes unbidden to of having come partly to. When in the end unbidden they open they are met by this dull white. Further one cannot.

On.

No knowledge of where gone from. Nor of how. Nor of whom. None of whence come to. Partly to. Nor of how. Nor of whom. None of anything. Save dimly of having come to. Partly to. With dread of being again. Partly again. Somewhere again. Somehow again. Someone again. Dim dread born first of consciousness alone. Dim consciousness alone. Confirmed when in the end the eyes unbidden open. To this dull white. By this dull white. Further one cannot.

On.

Dim consciousness first alone. Of mind alone. Alone come to. Partly to. Then worse come of body too. At the sight of this dull white of body too. Too come to. Partly to. When in the end the eyes unbidden open. To this dull white. Further one –

On.

Something of one come to. Somewhere to. Somehow to. First mind alone. Something of mind alone. Then worse come body too. Something of body too. When in the end the eyes unbidden open. To this dull white. Further –

On.

Dull with breath. Endless breath. Endless ending breath. Dread darling sight.

what is the word

folly –
folly for to –
for to –
what is the word –
folly from this –
all this –
folly from all this –
given –
folly given all this –
seeing –
folly seeing all this –
this –
what is the word –
this this –
this this here –
all this this here –
folly given all this –
seeing –
folly seeing all this this here –
for to –
what is the word –
see –
glimpse –
seem to glimpse –

need to seem to glimpse –

folly for to need to seem to glimpse –

what –

what is the word –

and where –

folly for to need to seem to glimpse what where –

where –

what is the word –

there –

over there –

away over there –

afar –

afar away over there –

afaint –

afaint afar away over there what –

what –

what is the word –

seeing all this –

all this this –

all this this here –

folly for to see what –

glimpse –

seem to glimpse –

need to seem to glimpse –

afaint afar away over there what –

folly for to need to seem to glimpse afaint afar away
    over there what –

what –
what is the word –

what is the word

Appendix

Heard in the Dark 1

The last time you went out the snow lay on the ground. You now lying in the dark stand that morning on the sill having pulled the door gently to behind you. You lean back against the door with bowed head making ready to set out. By the time you open your eyes your feet have disappeared and the skirts of your greatcoat come to rest on the surface of the snow. The dark scene seems lit from below. You see yourself at that last outset leaning against the door with closed eyes waiting for the word from you to go. You? To be gone. Then the snowlit scene. You lie in the dark with closed eyes and see yourself there as described making ready to strike out and away across the expanse of light. You hear again the click of the door pulled gently to and the silence before the steps can start. Next thing you are on your way across the white pasture afrolic with lambs in spring and strewn with red placentae. You take the course you always take which is a beeline for the gap or ragged point in the quickset that forms the western fringe. Thither from your entering the pasture you need normally from eighteen hundred to two thousand paces depending on your humour and the state of the ground. But on this last morning many more will be

necessary. Many many more. The beeline is so familiar to your feet that if necessary they could keep to it
and you sightless with error on arrival of not more
than a few feet north or south. And indeed without
any such necessity unless from within this is what
they normally do and not only here. For you advance
if not with closed eyes though this as often as not at
least with them fixed on the momentary ground
before your feet. That is all of nature you have seen.
Since you finally bowed your head. The fleeting
ground before your feet. From time to time. You do
not count your steps any more. For the simple reason
they number each day the same. Average day in day
out the same. The way being always the same. You
keep count of the days and every tenth night multiply. And add. Your father's shade is not with you any
more. It fell out long ago. You do not hear your footfalls any more. Unhearing unseeing you go your way.
Day after day. The same way. As if there were no
other any more. For you there is no other any more.
You used never to halt except to make your reckoning. So as to plod on from nought anew. This need
removed as we have seen there is none in theory to
halt any more. Save perhaps a moment at the outermost point. To gather yourself together for the
return. And yet you do. As never before. Not for
tiredness. You are no more tired now than you always

were. Not because of age. You are no older now than you always were. And yet you halt as never before. So that the same hundred yards you used to cover in a matter of three to four minutes may now take you anything from fifteen to twenty. The foot falls unbidden in midstep or next for lift cleaves to the ground bringing the body to a stand. Then a speechlessness whereof the gist, Can they go on? Or better, Shall they go on? The barest gist. Stilled when finally as always hitherto they do. You lie in the dark with closed eyes and see the scene. As you could not at the time. The dark cope of sky. The dazzling land. You at a standstill in the midst. The quarterboots sunk to the tops. The skirts of the greatcoat resting on the snow. In the old bowed head in the old block hat speechless misgiving. Halfway across the pasture on your beeline to the gap. The unerring feet fast. You look behind you as you could not then and see their trail. A great swerve. Withershins. Almost as if all at once the heart too heavy. In the end too heavy.

Heard in the Dark 2

Bloom of adulthood. Try a whiff of that. On your back in the dark you remember. Ah you you remember. Cloudless May day. She joins you in the little summerhouse. Entirely of logs. Both larch and fir. Six feet across. Eight from floor to vertex. Area twenty-four square feet to furthest decimal. Two small multicoloured lights vis-à-vis. Small stained diamond panes. Under each a ledge. There on summer Sundays after his midday meal your father loved to retreat with *Punch* and a cushion. The waist of his trousers unbuttoned he sat on the one ledge and turned the pages. You on the other your feet dangling. When he chuckled you tried to chuckle too. When his chuckle died yours too. That you should try to imitate his chuckle pleased and amused him greatly and sometimes he would chuckle for no other reason than to hear you try to chuckle too. Sometimes you turn your head and look out through a rose-red pane. You press your little nose against the pane and all without is rosy. The years have flown and there at the same place as then you sit in the bloom of adulthood bathed in rainbow light gazing before you. She is late. You close your eyes and try to calculate the volume. Simple sums you find a help in times of trouble. A haven. You arrive in the end at seven cubic yards approximately. Even still in the timeless dark you find figures a comfort. You assume a certain heart rate and reckon how many thumps a day. A week. A month. A year. And assuming a certain lifetime a lifetime. Till the last thump. But for the moment with hardly more than seventy American billion behind you you sit in the little summerhouse working out the volume. Seven cubic yards approximately. This strikes you for some reason as improbable and you set about your sum anew. But you have not got very far when her light step is heard. Light for a woman of her size. You open with quickening pulse your eyes and a moment later that seems an eternity her face appears at the window. Mainly blue in this position the natural pallor you so admire as indeed from it no doubt wholly blue your own. For natural pallor is a property you have in common. The violet lips do not return your smile. Now this window being flush with your eyes from where you sit and the floor as near as no matter with the outer ground you cannot but wonder if she has not sunk to her knees. Knowing from experience that the height or length you have in common is the sum of equal segments. For when bolt upright or lying at full stretch you cleave front to front then your knees touch and your pubes and the hairs of your heads mingle. Does it follow from this that the loss of height for the body that sits is the same as for it that kneels? At this point assuming level of seat adjustable as in the case of certain piano stools you close your eyes the better with mental measure to measure and compare the first and second segments namely from sole to kneepad and thence to pelvic girdle. How given you were both moving and at rest to the closed eye in your waking hours! By day and by night. To that perfect dark. That shadowless light. Simply to be gone. Or for affair as now. A single leg appears. Seen from above. You separate the segments and lay them side by side. It is as you half surmised. The upper is the longer and the sitter's loss the greater when seat at knee level. You leave the pieces lying there and open your eyes to find her sitting before you. All dead still. The ruby lips do not return your smile. Your gaze moves down to the breasts. You do not remember them so big. To the abdomen. Same impression. Dissolve to your father's straining against the unbuttoned waistband. Can it be she is with child without your having asked for as much as her hand? You go back into your mind. She too did you but know it has closed her eyes. So you sit face to face in the little summerhouse. With eyes closed and hands on knees. In the bloom of your adulthood. In that rainbow light. That dead still.

144